I0729855

by

# MELANIE HEPBURN

*For the big girls who just want to be carried by a strong man.*

Ebook ISBN: 978-1-7638087-8-2

Paperback ISBN: 978-1-7638087-1-3

Alternate cover paperback ISBN: 978-1-7638087-9-9



This story, all names, characters, and incidents portrayed in this production are from the author's imagination. Any identification with actual persons (living or deceased), places, buildings, and products is entirely coincidental.

The author does not provide consent for any part of this book to be used in the training of generative artificial intelligence. AI was not used in the creation of this work.

Cover design by Red Light Graphic Design

Alternate Cover design by Melanie Hepburn

Alternate Cover Image from Deposit Photos

Cover photography by Lindee Robinson Photography

Developmental Editing by Morgan Waddle

Line Editing by Shana Grogan

Proof Reading by the best proof reader in the world (i.e.: the author's husband)

The author acknowledges Whadjuk Nyoongar people as the traditional owners of the land on which this work was written. She pays her respects to the people, cultures and elders both past and present.

# Contents

# Chapter One

**Charlie**

If you thought Charlotte Sinclair, the daughter of the CEO of one of New York's biggest property development companies, had never known hard work, you'd be forgiven. Most of her colleagues at Sinclair Properties certainly thought so. She was determined to prove them wrong.

Cape Wilde was the best chance she had at proving to her father—and to all his gossiping staff— that she was worthy of becoming his heir. All she had to do was buy the perfect parcel of land for the next Sinclair Properties development—a luxury resort— something even her father had failed at.

It was beautiful here, and a resort in coastal Maine would be the perfect place for visitors to relax and enjoy a break from the busyness of life in Boston or New York.

Charlie had arrived in Cape Wilde that afternoon, and felt an immediate glow of affection for the little town. It was perfect. The main street, with its glass-fronted shops with flowers in window boxes, enticed her to stop and browse. She'd arrived a little too late for that, and looked wistfully at the artistic displays in the windows. Maybe tomorrow. She parked her rental and turned the engine off.

Shopping would have to wait until she'd taken care of business. All she had to do was convince the owner of the land to sell it to her, and she'd be on her way back to New York, triumphant. She grinned in satisfaction at the thought of her father being stunned that she'd closed the deal on the land he'd had his eye on for years. Her colleagues would have to be impressed. She would finally earn their respect and maybe they'd stop whispering about her when they thought she couldn't hear.

Not one of them believed she was capable of more than the most basic of tasks. Because that's all her father had ever trusted her with. Until now. This was her chance. For once, her father had given her a job that could actually impact the business. She wanted to prove she was more than just a trust fund socialite. The most she'd ever been encouraged to do in her 26 years was attend charity galas and art exhibitions. She snorted. It was all for show.

The reality was much less enviable. A motherless child craving her workaholic father's attention didn't gain sympathy when your family had as much money as the Sinclairs. But having money didn't mean being happy.

Charlie sighed as she parked her rental and rested her head on the steering wheel, her long brown hair falling forward to hide her face like a curtain.

She lifted her head from the steering wheel and pushed her hair back from her face. Rubbing her eyes, she stifled a yawn. The drive had been long, and she was starving. There would be plenty of work to do tomorrow, but for now she needed something to eat.

Charlie grabbed her handbag and got out of the car. The air was still warm, even in the early evening. She felt her shoulders relax a little as she breathed in the salty scent of the ocean. She turned, taking in the little town of Cape Wilde.

Main Street was quaint, lined with old timber buildings, the shops displaying their wares in the windows. Signs hung over the doorways, swinging gently in the breeze. Brightly colored flowers added a dash of color, and a faint, soft sweetness to the air.

Not a single piece of litter was to be seen, nor an overflowing trash can. A real estate agent's window drew Charlie's eye. She walked over to look at the offerings. Each property was listed on a printout, with a hand-written note on the bottom giving the agent's suggestion for who might like it most.

She smiled as she read the cards. The personal note was a nice touch.

The land she had come to Cape Wilde to buy wasn't listed, which she was thankful for.

Less competition that way.

Giving the window one last look, she turned on her heel and made her way down the gentle slope towards a bar that had caught her eye.

She pushed open the door of Wilde Brews'n'Blues, the expected sound of blues music filling the air. Charlie walked inside slowly, taking the time to look around as she did.

It was a craft brewery, with a bar to one side and a large deck overlooking the water. As you sat at the bar, you could watch the brewers at work, although nobody was working around the shining equipment right now. The place was busy, but not packed, and she was suddenly doubly thankful that she'd changed from her usual tailored business suit and stiletto pumps to more comfortable clothing for the drive. She felt much more herself in jeans, a plain white tank top, and a bright pink, lightweight cardigan over the top.

She would have stood out like a sore thumb in her

usual work clothes. Charlie smoothed her hand down over the denim of her jeans and hitched her oversized purse on her shoulder.

The bar seemed like the obvious place to start as there wasn't a greeter—it didn't seem to be a place where people stood on ceremony—and she was hungry.

She marched over to the bar and slid onto a stool, dropping her bag onto the empty seat next to her with a thump.

"What have you got in that thing? Rocks?" A deep voice drawled from beside her in amusement.

Charlie gave a surprised squeak and twisted to look behind her, almost falling off her seat. The owner of the voice was a tall, broad man with dark brown hair that was cropped close at the sides and longer on top. He stood behind her in the nearby doorway, leaning one shoulder against the frame with his arms crossed over his chest.

Worn denim jeans encased his thick thighs, mud splattered where they met his equally muddy boots. His flannel shirt was faded from wear, the sleeves rolled up over muscled forearms, the front open to show a black t-shirt. A very tight black t-shirt that did nothing to hide his muscular torso.

Charlie's eyes drifted up to his face. Dark lashes framed intense blue eyes, over which one of his thick brown brows lifted quizzically. But it was when her eyes met his and he grinned that she stopped breathing. Eyes sparkling, a dimple appeared in his cheek.

Holy fuck. Whoever this guy was, he was sex on legs. Charlie squeezed her thighs together, swallowing the lump that had formed in her throat.

"So?" He asked.

Charlie blinked. He'd asked her something, hadn't he? She turned a little further on the seat to face him fully, but lost her balance.

With a squeak, she slid off the chair and braced herself to hit the ground, eyes squeezed shut. But strong arms wrapped around her instead, pulling her against his firm chest.

# Chapter Two

**Rhett**

After back-to-back multi-day guided hikes, Rhett West was beyond tired. Working for weeks on end without a break used to invigorate him, but the last year or two had been exhausting.

Be your own boss, they said. It would be fun, they said. He grunted and shook his head as he climbed the short flight of stairs to the deck that ran along three sides of Wilde Brews'n'Blues.

Rhett stopped by the side door into the main bar, taking a moment to scrape the dried mud off his boots. Mud was an occupational hazard for a man who was the owner and primary guide of Cape Wilde Outdoor Adventures.

The peak summer tourist season had only just

begun, and Rhett was already exhausted. All he wanted was to get a bite to eat, shower, and sleep for a week.

Satisfied that his boots wouldn't leave mud all over the floor, he pushed open the door and stepped inside. He didn't make it more than a pace into the bar before he pulled up short, stunned into stillness by the woman who was crossing the space towards him.

*Well, hello.*

She was like sunshine after a week of rain. Long, glossy brown hair spilled over her shoulders in a tumble. She hadn't seen him yet, approaching the near-empty bar as if on a mission.

She was shorter than him—not that it was hard. At well over six feet, Rhett towered over almost everyone he knew. She would fit perfectly in his arms.

Wow, where had that thought come from? He flexed his hands to get himself under control. What was wrong with him? He was never like this. He wasn't a sailor, and she wasn't a siren calling him to his doom, no matter how beautiful.

And she was beautiful.

He shifted from foot to foot, resenting his lack of control. Rhett West was nothing if not always in control.

*Not right now.*

He grunted in frustration, intending to ignore the

woman who was obviously from out of town. Probably a holiday maker here with her family. She had that polished city look, despite the sneakers and jeans she wore. Her bag thudded onto the seat beside her, and he couldn't help himself, saying the first thing that came into his head.

"What have you got in that thing? Rocks?"

*Oh, real smooth. No wonder she's staring at you like you've got horns.*

She slid off the barstool with an adorable squeak, and he couldn't let her fall, so he covered the short distance between them and gathered her in his arms.

She was all soft curves and perfume, just the right amount of floral without smelling like a department store. Her hands had come up to rest against his chest, her nails painted a pink that could only be described as 'intense'. The color suited her. As if she was daring anyone to comment on her choice.

Rhett smiled ruefully as he held her against his chest, sliding one arm up to cradle her head. He closed his eyes and breathed in the scent of her shampoo. He'd never smell jasmine again without thinking of her. He knew that as clearly as he knew his own name.

"Oh!" she exclaimed in a breathy voice that sent a jolt of heat to his groin. Is that what she'd sound like when she came?

He swallowed and opened his eyes. Jaw clenched,

he put her gently back on her feet and stepped away. His hands slid down her arms from her shoulders to her wrists, as if he couldn't bear losing contact with her.

"I promise I'm not normally this clumsy," she said, stepping back to let her go. She brushed her hands on her jeans, her cheeks pink.

Rhett watched as she fussed with her hair, smoothing the strands and putting herself to rights.

This was a woman who just got on with things. The world moved on, and she wasn't about to let it move on without her. He smiled, preparing to wish her well and walk away, but she reached out and put a small hand on his forearm, stalling him.

He looked down at her hand; the pink painted nails standing out against his tanned skin.

*No engagement ring. No wedding band.*

He blinked, still staring at her hand. She snatched it back.

"I'm sorry. I should have thought..." she said, trailing off.

Her eyes were a golden brown, almost amber, with darker flecks. They reminded him of the fall leaves that he loved so much.

"No." He managed say.

"No?" Her brows drew together.

He cleared his throat. "I mean, no need to apologize." He waved his hand towards the seat next to her. "Do you mind if I?"

She nodded. Then frowned and shook her head. "No, I don't mind. Um, here." She dragged her bag off the seat, dumping it unceremoniously on the floor.

Rhett's lips twitched, but he sat, watching her as she sat carefully.

"Hey Rhett."

He turned to see his cousin, Mason, limping towards him, the perpetual scowl he wore deepening as he took in the woman sitting next to him.

"Mason," he replied, straightening in his seat.

"Who's your date?"

"She's not—"

"Oh, we're not—"

Rhett's lips twitched. Mason just grunted and shook his head, moving to the far end of the bar and hoisting himself onto an empty barstool.

"Not very friendly, is he?" she asked.

He whipped his head towards her, ready with an angry retort to defend Mason, but there was no animosity in her expression.

"Yeah, well, being in pain all the time will probably do that," he said, but smiled to soften the words.

She chewed on her bottom lip and looked at her lap.

"What can I get you, ma'am? Rhett?"

He didn't bother telling old Errol the bartender they weren't on a date. In a town as small as Cape Wilde, everyone would know by this time tomorrow that he'd been seen with a beautiful stranger. If he protested, it would be even more damning.

Rhett waited while she ordered, then gave his own order, paying for both their drinks.

"I can pay for my drink."

"Never said you couldn't." Rhett took a long pull from his beer, closing his eyes as the refreshing cold brew slid down his throat. The tension in his shoulders eased a little, and he sighed, rolling his head on his neck to stretch out some kinks that had developed carrying a pack for the last few days.

He glanced over at her to see her swirling her wineglass absentmindedly, the way he'd seen the folk who fancied themselves as wine connoisseurs do at the fine dining restaurant over at Calamity Cove. But with her, it didn't look contrived. It looked practiced, like she'd spent a lot of time in fancy restaurants of the like not found outside of a big city.

"Where are you from?" He surprised himself by asking.

"New York," she said simply, taking a sip of her wine as she glanced at him from under lowered lashes.

"Ahh," he replied, setting one booted foot on the ground, the other on the rung of the barstool.

She lifted an eyebrow in question. "What's that supposed to mean?"

Rhett shrugged. "You don't look like you're from around here."

She looked down at her clothes. "I don't?"

He couldn't help but laugh. "Nope."

He held his hand out to her. "I'm Rhett."

Her grip was surprisingly firm, and he enjoyed the feel of her soft fingers against his callused ones more than he cared to admit.

"Charlie."

It suited her. "Nice to meet you, Charlie. Want to join me for dinner?"

She laughed, caught by surprise. "I can't do that."

"Why not?"

She opened her mouth and then snapped it shut. "Actually, sure. Okay, I'll join you for dinner."

Rhett's face split open into a wide grin. Charlie smiled back.

They found a table outside on the lawn to one side of the building, lit by lights strung between trees. The moonlight cast a glow over the dark water, the sound of waves lapping against the rocky shore a familiar, calming sound.

If they'd actually been on a date, it couldn't have been more romantic.

A moonlit evening, a singer crooning blues over the

diners, and a woman who turned out to be as interesting to talk to as she was beautiful.

Rhett forgot all about being tired, or the work that was waiting for him tomorrow. He didn't want this evening with Charlie to end.

"Where are you staying?" He asked as they were finishing cups of coffee after their meal. The blues singer had long since packed up, and the only staff left were cleaning the inside tables.

She shot him a sharp glance, and he lifted his hands as if defending against a blow.

"Whoa! Not asking so I can get into your pants, Charlie." Although he wasn't opposed to the idea. Did she even think about him like that? He gave himself a mental shake.

*Get a grip. It's only been a few hours. She's just after some company.*

Charlie stifled a yawn behind her hand and then gave him a rueful smile. "That's a shame. I wouldn't mind getting into yours."

Rhett had, unfortunately, chosen just that moment to swallow the last of his coffee and choked. He fought to not splutter too badly, but failed dismally.

She started laughing and stood up to pat him on the back as he cleared his throat. "Did I take you by surprise?"

He turned to straddle the bench seat and face her,

which put him level with her breasts. And dear god, she had glorious breasts. All night he'd fought not to stare, but now he gave in to temptation. They were big, but not out of proportion to the rest of her deliciously curvy body, and he bet they were gloriously soft and fit just perfectly in his hands.

"Eyes are up here, buddy."

He flushed, dragging his attention away from her chest to her face. She was smirking at him, one eyebrow cocked.

"Can I get your number?"

She smiled. "Sure, but I'm only in town for a few days."

"Oh." A spike of disappointment ran through him. He gave a mental shrug. He'd enjoyed her company and that would have to be enough.

He did have a problem though. There was absolutely no way Rhett would be able to stand without Charlie seeing exactly what effect she had on him. He shifted slightly on the bench.

"Rhett, I like you. You're cute and fun. I think we both know where this could go, right?" She reached out and touched the side of his face, brushing her thumb over his lower lip.

He nodded and turned his head to nip at her digit, soothing the bite with his tongue. Her mouth dropped open slightly, her tongue darting out to wet her bottom lip. He groaned and tugged her towards him, sliding his hands around her waist.

He'd never been so turned inside out by a woman. And never in such a short amount of time. Maybe he'd been wrong and she did want what he did? He'd take whatever she was willing to give.

Charlie's hands gripped his shoulders, bracing herself as she shifted to straddle his lap.

Perfect. He had her exactly where he wanted her. Deliciously soft curves pressed against him and he fought to keep his breathing even as desire flooded him.

"I'm not too heavy?" She asked, a line forming between her brows.

He growled. "You're perfect." His hands gripped her backside and squeezed, dragging her forward until she was pressed up against his hard cock.

Right at that moment, he wanted to curse whoever had invented clothing.

She smiled, sliding a hand between them to stroke her fingertips lightly over the denim-clad bulge in his pants. He almost came at the contact, burying his face in her neck and nipping her with his teeth.

She giggled and sighed, dropping her head to one side. "You're a biter, huh?"

In answer, he nipped her again before trailing kisses up her neck and capturing her lips with his own.

# Chapter Three

**Charlie**

Charlie was bouncing as she made her way along Cape Wilde's Main Street a few days later, coffee in hand. She couldn't wipe the smile from her face.

She'd seen Rhett every day. Picnics by the ocean. Boat trips to see the puffins that migrated to the area. Drives to nearby towns to the many markets that seemed to be a constant fixture in the holiday season. Every chance Rhett could get away from work, he spent with her. And she, in return, put off her real reason for being in Cape Wilde.

But she couldn't put it off anymore. She tried to put Rhett out of her mind. She needed to focus on the offer she was about to make to the owner of the land she intended to buy. But, try as she might, her thoughts drifted back to Rhett.

Despite the way their first meeting had gone, Rhett had insisted that they take things slowly. He knew she was only there for a little while, and she figured she could always visit again. It was a bit of a drive from New York, but she never took her PTO. It might be nice to have somewhere—and someone—to visit. And when the resort project started, she'd see if she could get on the team. Then she'd see him almost every day.

She grinned, imagining the future with her hottie outdoorsman by her side. It was almost as if she could feel Rhett's large hands on her. His touch was like fire, lighting her up inside in ways she had thought were long dead.

Charlie liked her curves, and she wasn't ashamed of her body. But that didn't mean she was immune to nasty comments. She had once been set up on a blind date, only to have the guy tell her he was sorry, but she was too fat for him. Her father constantly commented on everything she ate as a teenager until she stopped eating in front of him, which wasn't particularly hard considering how much he worked.

And even the supposedly friendly comments could get to her. Like the woman in her spin class at the gym telling her how much of an inspiration she was for working out in a sports bra. But she didn't say that to any of the size four women in the class who were doing the same.

So when Rhett looked at her as if she was the most gorgeous woman he'd ever laid eyes on, she had bloomed inside. She couldn't wait to see him again tonight after he finished work.

The few times they'd talked about work, she'd said she was in investments in New York, which was what she usually said when she didn't want people to judge her for her money. Sinclair Properties was so well known on the east coast that it never took long for people to treat her differently. And she didn't want Rhett to treat her differently.

He said he worked in the family business, something about doing tours of the local area. Considering the odd hours he worked, that made sense to Charlie. She didn't push, knowing he'd tell her more when he was ready.

So she'd saved his number into her phone as 'Cape Wilde Cutie', which had him blushing when she'd shown him. It seemed like Mr. Sex-on-legs was a little under appreciated, which she planned to rectify. Over and over again.

He was all broad shoulders and piercing blue eyes that seemed to see into her soul. When he smiled and that dimple appeared in his left cheek, her stomach flip-flopped.

She took a deep breath and huffed it out, trying to focus. Charlie's ponytail swung back and forth as she strode up the street, this time in ballet flats and a cherry red wrap dress that made her feel like she belonged in the 1940s. The fabric had white polka dots on it, and a little frill at the neck where the deep vee crossed over to tie at her hip. She'd worn her favorite red lipstick to match, her large tote with her laptop and folio inside slung over her shoulder.

She mentally ran over the proposal she'd prepared. It was a good one, an offer above market value, but within her father's allowed budget for the project. All things going to plan, she could get the paperwork signed today and then have a few more days to enjoy her stay in the town.

A few more days to enjoy spending with Rhett.

She took a sip of her coffee, sighing. It was delicious, a surprise considering she'd never really had passable coffee outside New York. The man who served her every day at Wilde Buns—the name of the bakery that had her lips twitching in amusement—had even remembered her order.

Charlie stopped in front of a rundown shop and glanced at the address on her phone calendar. 'Cape Wilde Outdoor Adventures' was painted on the glass window in faded colors. It was the right place, and it looked like the owner wasn't having a good time of it, going by the peeling paint.

She glanced down the street at the other shop fronts, cheery pots of flowers flanking the steps and bright displays in the windows. Frowning, she compared them to the empty pots with stubbed out cigarette butts instead of plants, and a shop window apparently used to store old archive boxes.

Maybe the owner would be happy to sell the land to her? Her father hadn't succeeded, but times changed. It certainly looked like they could use the money. Only one way to find out, she figured, pushing the door open on squeaky hinges, the bell attached to the door jangling loudly.

The dusty interior could really do with some work, she thought as she examined the mountain of camping gear stacked in the corner and what had obviously once been a reception desk but was now piled high with guidebooks and maps that teetered precariously.

The sound of booted footsteps had Charlie turning, a polite smile on her face. Until Rhett walked into the room, wiping his hands on a rag.

Broad shoulders stretched the fabric of his flannel shirt, which was unbuttoned over a white tee shirt. A very tight white tee shirt that did nothing to hide his muscular torso. It was his uniform, she'd discovered. Flannel and denim. She didn't hate it at all.

Besides, the man had muscles on top of muscles and there was something about a broad-shouldered man in butt-hugging jeans that made her knees weak.

The sleeves of his shirt were rolled up over broad forearms, and as he folded his arms over his chest, her gaze jumped to his face.

"Morning, what can I—" he broke off as he looked and saw her. He smiled and tilted his head. "Charlie? What are you doing here?"

At first, Charlie wondered if she'd made a mistake, but no, she'd definitely come to the right place. Was Cape Wilde Outdoor Adventures the family business Rhett had said he worked at? She'd just have to ask Rhett where the owner was.

"Um, hi Rhett. I wanted to speak to Henry West," she said, pulling the folio out of her tote to give herself something to do.

"Henry West?" Rhett's smile fell, and his eyes focused on her folio with suspicion.

She took a step closer and his eyes—those intense blue eyes she'd drowned in last night—snapped to hers.

"Yes, he's the owner, isn't he? I wanted to talk to him about the land out at—"

Rhett's hands tightened into fists. "The land. You're here about the land."

"That's right. I work for Sinclair Properties—"

Rhett closed his eyes and laughed, but it was bitter and humorless. "I should have known."

This was not going well at all.

"Sorry?"

He shook his head. "I knew it was too good to be true."

"What was?"

"You."

His blue eyes were so fiercely angry that she took an involuntary step back.

"I knew you were too good to be true."

"I don't understand." Charlie's head was swimming. What was he talking about?

"Let me explain then, beautiful."

The endearment did not sound at all complimentary and she flinched.

"Henry was my grandfather. He died and left me the business. I own the land. But you knew that already, didn't you?"

"What? No!"

He shook his head, crossing his arms in front of his broad chest. "Don't deny it. You people have been trying to get us to sell for years. For what? To knock down all the trees and build some huge resort that would kill the atmosphere of our town? Let alone what it would do for the local environment. Not going to happen."

Charlie's chest clenched. He really thought the worst of her. That she'd come here to what, seduce him into selling the land? She felt sick at the thought. Of all the things her father had done, there's no way he'd stoop to prostituting his daughter to get a deal.

*You told your father you'd do anything to prove you belonged in the business.*

She cringed.

"No, Rhett. I didn't come here to seduce you into selling the land."

He scoffed and looked to one side, refusing to meet her eyes.

She closed the distance between them, lifting a hand towards him and then dropping it when he flinched away. "I'm the same person—"

He laughed again, and she ground her teeth in frustration.

"—despite what you think of my father's company."

He turns on her, staring daggers at her. "You're Sinclair's daughter?"

Oh, that was a mistake. She grimaced and nodded.

"Your father—" he almost spat the word "—would come to town every year or two, trying to bribe my grandfather to sell the land. Pop had the same answer that I do. No."

She felt torn. This deal had to work, or she'd lose

everything she'd worked so hard for. But all her daydreams about a future with Rhett were slipping through her fingers, too. There had to be a way she could make this work, or she'd lose Rhett and her father would never give her any responsibility again.

"Look, this time it's me, not him, and there's a different proposal. Would you just look—"

Rhett smiled like a predator. "Oh no, beautiful. I've been running this business since I was fifteen years old. Trust me when I say there will never be a deal with your dad."

Charlie blinks up at him, not sure what to say. This has not gone at all like she'd planned. It felt like someone had taken her entire world, turned it upside down and was shaking it. How had everything gone so wrong?

"Will you at least look at the offer?" She tried again, her tone pleading as she held out the folio, expecting him to take it from her hands. His lips pressed together in a thin line and his gaze was icy. She stepped back and let go of the folio, but he didn't take it.

She watched as the contents fluttered to the ground, paper spilling around his feet like all her lost hopes and dreams.

Her father will never let her take on anything of

importance. She'll never be his heir. She would always be the unworthy daughter.

"Get out," Rhett practically snarled.

Charlie reared back at the venom in his tone. Biting her lip, she tried one more time. "Rhett, I—"

"I said get out!" He didn't shout, but it was a near thing. The tendons in his neck strained and he was practically spitting with anger.

Charlie turned and darted for the door, barely hearing the cheery jangle of the bell as she made her escape.

# Chapter Four

**Rhett**

The rest of the day went in a blur. Rhett hadn't bothered to pick up the papers where they'd fallen from Charlie's hand that morning. He'd just turned his back on them and gone back to work. He was repairing a tear in a tent's zipper when his cousin, Cassie, strolled into the workroom.

"Lunch, Rhett?" She said with a smile, turning down the speaker he'd been blasting rock music through. She held up two paper bags. "Chicken or beef?"

He lifted an eyebrow and put aside the canvas he was stitching.

"You have to ask?"

She laughed and handed him one of the bags. "Always worth a try. People change, you know."

Rhett knew his cousin far too well to believe this was a casual visit. He took the bag and pulled out a beef burger, closing his eyes as he breathed in the delicious aroma. He may as well enjoy the food while he waited for whatever it was she had to say.

"Didn't eat breakfast again, huh?" Cassie asked as she watched him from her perch on the edge of a crate.

She was wearing scrubs with octopus on them today. Bright pink scrubs with rainbow colored octopus. Rhett had lost count of how many pairs she had. She maintained that as a vet she got filthy so often she had to have multiple pairs on hand at work so she would look presentable.

He thought it was just a way to appease her cartoon animal loving side.

"Cute scrubs," he said between bites.

She smiled. "Thanks."

They ate in silence, the sounds of the music playing softly in the background. Cassie was the youngest of the West kids, and the only girl of five—six if you counted Rhett, and they did count Rhett as a brother more than a cousin.

When they'd finished eating, Rhett took their wrappers and tossed them in the bin in the corner.

"So, what can I do for you, Cassie?"

She titled her head to one side and pursed her lips. "Who is she?"

He knew it would be about Charlie. Just one time he wanted to make a mistake in this damned town and not have everyone know it.

"Who is who?" The only reason he stayed in the same room was he knew if he didn't, she'd just follow him, anyway. This way, the interrogation would be over quicker.

"The woman you've been seen with. Everyone who's been into the surgery this week can't stop talking about her," she smirked. "So, who is she?"

Rhett sighed and rubbed his hand over his face. "Nobody. She's nobody."

"Oh really? Old Errol said you had your tongue halfway down her throat and were practically fu—"

"Hey!" It didn't matter what was between him and Charlie, she didn't deserve to be spoken about like that.

"Oh?" Cassie was smirking.

Little stirrer. She always did like to cause trouble with her brothers.

"Look, Cassie. She's a Sinclair."

Cassie's smirk fell. "What?"

There were no secrets in the West family. They knew all about the plans of Sinclair Properties. Hell, most people in town knew, thanks to the development proposal Charlie's father had lodged a few years ago with the council.

"Yeah, exactly. I only found out this morning when she came to offer for the land."

Cassie pulled a face. "Oh, Rhett."

He grimaced. "Same old same, right? Out of town women just want me for my money." He choked out a laugh, but it was a poor attempt at humor. By the way Cassie gave him a sympathetic smile, he knew his hurt wasn't lost on her.

"Are you sure she's like Lisa?"

Rhett leaned back on his hands and sighed. "I don't know what to think."

That's what you got for losing your heart to a summer fling, only to have her leave town after telling you quite publicly that she was too good for a crappy little town like this. That was a long time ago, but it still smarted.

"What are they offering this time?"

"No idea. I didn't look."

Cassie shot him an incredulous look. "Seriously? Come on, Rhett. Aren't you curious?"

Rhett rolled his eyes. "The packet is on the floor in the shop, if you want to have a look."

Cassie gave a whoop and hopped down off the crate, padding into the shop in the crocs she wore when not in surgery. Rhett listened to the squeak of her shoes as she made her way to the front of the shop. He picked up the canvas tent again, resuming his stitching.

"Hey, Rhett?" She said as she walked back into the workroom.

"Hmm?" He said, squinting at the seam in his hands as he stitched it together neatly.

"Did you know she's staying in one of your cabins?"

"What?"

No way. There was no way Charlie could be staying in one of his rental cabins. Cassie laughed as she waved a piece of paper at him. He squinted at what looked like a hand-written note.

"Give it here," he said, holding out his hand.

Cassie handed it over, laughing. "One guess to where you'll be tonight."

Rhett scowled at her before running his eyes over the note. She *was* staying in one of the cabins that he rented out through the town's holiday letting agency.

On the exact land she was offering to buy. Of all the sneaky things she could have done.

He was on his feet and out the door, heading towards his truck before he realized where he was going.

"Want me to lock up for you?" Cassie called after him.

"Shit!" He stopped and ran a hand through his

hair. He couldn't go racing off to the cabin now. It was barely after lunch and there was no guarantee she would be there. He had her number, but damned if he was going to call her.

"No. I have bookings this afternoon." And that was the other thing. He had a business to run.

Rhett checked his watch. He couldn't leave for another five hours at least. It was going to be a long day.

It was dark by the time Rhett pulled up outside Charlie's cabin.

No, not Charlie's cabin. His cabin. As soon as she was packed and gone, life could get back to normal.

His truck's engine rumbled in the still air. A light flicked on over the small porch, the front door opening to reveal Charlie in leggings and a cream-colored wrap-around cardigan.

Rhett turned the engine off and climbed out of the truck, not wanting to delay this confrontation. Thunder rumbled in the distance, mirroring his mood.

She'd come here to take away the one thing he loved most. The peace and quiet of Cape Wilde. That monstrous resort that he'd seen the plans to would destroy everything he held dear.

He paused at the front of his truck, the light from inside the cabin throwing her into relief. He couldn't see her expression, but she had her arms crossed over her chest, tugging the cardigan tightly around her.

He stopped. The last thing he wanted to do was make her afraid, but how else would she feel? He was bigger than her. The cabin was in the woods with no neighbors that would hear if she screamed. And he had been very angry the last time they had spoken. Rhett ran a hand over his face, his anger deflating.

"Hi," he said, not stepping any closer to her.

"Hi."

The wind gusted, sending leaves blowing around his feet.

"This cabin is my favorite," he said. "It's where my grandfather and I used to stay when he took me fishing. On a clear day, you can see for miles out to sea."

She nodded. "It's a pretty spot."

Rhett rubbed his hand over the back of his neck. "Yeah."

They're both silent for a moment.

"What are you doing here?"

That was an excellent question. A few minutes ago he would have answered it with perfect certainty. He was there to tell her to leave and make sure she did. But now? He found he wanted to believe her. He wanted her to have not known who he was that first night. He wanted—

He wanted her.

"Did you really not know I owned the land?"

She nodded, her eyes unwavering as they met his. "I swear I didn't know."

"Alright," he said and gave a small smile. "I'm sorry for this morning. I reacted badly and I shouldn't have."

She nodded again, her arms relaxing so she was no longer hugging the cardigan tightly around her. Something loosened in Rhett's chest as she returned his smile with a small one of her own.

"It's ok. I can see how it would have looked." She scoffed and looked away. "Though I'm the last one anyone would have chosen as a femme fatale to seduce you out of your property."

Rhett's confusion must have shown when she darted a look at him.

"I mean, look at you," she waved her hand towards him, "and look at me." She gestured down her own body.

A bolt of lightning lit up the sky, followed almost immediately by a deafening crack of thunder that made them both flinch. Rain started falling and Rhett moved without thinking, dashing towards the doorway and ushering Charlie inside.

"It's not safe out here. Let's get inside," he said by way of explanation.

Anybody who spent as much time as he did outdoors knew to seek shelter when thunder followed lightning that quickly.

He stooped to unlace his boots and pulled them and his socks off, leaving them by the door, more out of something to do than habit.

"You're right, you know," he said. "I'm not good enough for you."

She blinked, her mouth dropping open. "That's not what I meant."

"You have money, Charlie. I don't."

She stepped towards him, her eyes shining. "That doesn't matter to me. It's never mattered to me."

Rhett ran a hand through his hair. "You can't say it doesn't change things."

She sighed and turned away, shaking her head slightly. "You never said what you were doing here."

Rhett straightened and looked around the cabin. The floor plan of the cabin was roughly square, with one room for the living and dining area, shaped like the letter L. In the corner there was a bedroom that held a cast-iron bed big enough for two. Next to it was a small bathroom with doors to both the bedroom and the main area.

Charlie curled up in one of the two overstuffed

armchairs, her feet tucked underneath her legs. She must have been reading when he arrived as there was a book face down on the side table next to her chair.

"To be honest, I was coming to kick you out."

She barked out a laugh. "Considering this cabin is yours, I'm not surprised."

He scuffed his bare foot on the floor and looked cautiously at her. "Yeah?"

The wind howled outside, rain lashing at the windows.

"Come and sit down. I can't imagine you'll be going anywhere for a while."

Rhett went to the window and peered into the dark. "This storm has come in fast." His phone beeped, and he pulled it from his pocket, swiping at the screen to open up a weather alert with a frown.

"What's wrong?"

Rhett took a moment to answer. "I don't like the idea of driving in this," he said, his voice gravelly. He stalked to the French doors that open onto the small ocean-facing deck and stepped outside.

Charlie got up to follow him and gasped as she spied the sky over the ocean. Dark and foreboding, and she shivered as the wind picked up further, sending salty spray into the air. Her hair was blown around her face, as the trees were whipped into a frenzy by the violent wind.

"So you wait out the storm out here," she said. Lightning streaked across the sky. A roll of thunder boomed so loudly she clapped her hands over her ears and shrieked.

Rhett ushered her back inside, pulling the doors shut behind them. He cursed under his breath and raked a hand over his face. "Yeah, I'll have to wait here." But he didn't sound happy about it.

"This cabin has surely weathered lots of storms," Charlie said.

Rhett barked out a laugh, lifting his head to the ceiling and shaking his head, hands on his hips. "That's not the problem."

"Oh?"

"The weather service is predicting it won't clear until morning."

She blinked up at him. "So you'll stay until morning."

He stepped towards her. "You're still not seeing the problem, beautiful."

"So tell me."

He hesitated before meeting her confused amber gaze. "Charlie, there's only one bed."

# Chapter Five

## Charlie

He was right. There was only one bed. There wasn't even a couch, just a couple of armchairs that weren't that comfortable for sitting in, so she couldn't imagine trying to sleep in one.

Charlie looked towards the bedroom. This morning she'd hoped that's where they'd end up tonight. But the animosity Rhett had shown towards her when he'd realized who she was changed things, even if he had apologized and calmed down.

She sighed and headed back to her armchair and the abandoned glass of wine. She sank onto the seat, trying to get comfortable and failing dismally. The sounds of the storm raging outside making her jumpy.

"Did you purposely find the most uncomfortable

chairs for this cabin?" She asked, stuffing a cushion against one hip to stop the hard wood of the arm from digging into her butt.

Rhett laughed, the sound so unexpected that she gave a little jump. Her eyes shot to his, watching as he padded on bare feet to the other armchair, draping himself on the seat in a way that reminded her of a king on his throne.

He lifted a hand and ran his fingers through his hair, the tee shirt he was wearing stretching over his broad chest. Dear god, he was stunning. Charlie felt her breath catch as she took him in. Legs splayed open, his thighs stretching the denim tight.

She remembered what it felt like to be riding on top of those thighs, his hands gripping her. Squeezing her as if he couldn't get enough of her. She shifted slightly in her seat, heat pooling between her legs. It was becoming harder and harder to remember that she didn't want to have sex with him.

She didn't. She really didn't.

It would be a bad idea. A really really bad idea.

He smirked, one side of his mouth kicking up and a dimple appearing in his cheek. That damned dimple! Why did he have to have them? She'd always found dimples irresistible.

One of his hands was gripping the back of the armchair behind his head, the other draped casually over his thigh. He reached down and cupped the bulge in his pants, and she jerked her eyes away.

Oh god, she'd been staring! How embarrassing.

"You can keep looking, beautiful. I don't mind at all." His voice was a deep drawl that sent shivers over her skin.

She looked away and harrumphed, eliciting a laugh from him.

Charlie needed to get control of the situation. She was here for a reason, and she needed to get the job done.

"Did you read the proposal?" She asked.

His formerly casual expression shuttered to something unreadable, and he shifted to lean forward, elbows resting on his knees. "No."

It was her turn to smirk. "Let me guess. You left the whole folio on the floor."

He grunted, his lips pressed into a thin line. She felt a rush of sympathy at his situation. It mustn't be easy running the type of business he ran. It was seasonal and physically demanding. Getting qualified help in a small town would be difficult unless someone was willing to move to the area.

"It's not about the money for you, is it?" Her head tilted to one side in consideration. Most people didn't have a clue what it was like to be her. All they saw was the money. Sure, she'd not wanted for anything material her entire childhood. She'd gone to the best schools and had everything she could ask for. The latest clothes, music, a new car every birthday after she got her license. She had been the envy of all her friends, though it was difficult to call the people she was forced to associate with because of who their parents were, 'friends'. During college she'd had a blissful two weeks living in the dorms like a normal person until someone found out who her father was.

When she'd gained control of her trust fund at 21 years old—not needing to work a day in her life—she vowed *she'd not touch a cent*. And she hadn't in the five years since. Charlotte Sinclair might have the world at her fingertips, according to most, but she wanted to earn her way through life, not buy it.

Rhett's expression shifted, his lids heavy with dark shadows under eyes rimmed in red. He sighed and rubbed his neck, stifling a yawn. He sat back in his chair, shifting to throw a leg over one arm as if he'd long ago figured out how to sit comfortably in them. She supposed he had, if the furniture hadn't changed since he'd come here as a boy with his grandfather to go fishing. Which it looked like it hadn't.

Charlie smiled at the thought, watching Rhett as he watched her. The silence wasn't uncomfortable. He nodded, as if finally coming to some internal decision.

"No, it's not about the money."

Charlie smiled in what she hoped was encouragement. "Then what is it?"

"Why?" Rhett's eyes narrowed. "I'm not going to sell, so you don't have to feign interest."

Charlie's smile fell. "You really don't think much of me, do you?" She pulled her knees to her chest and wrapped her arms around them, hugging herself to ward off the sudden chill that had nothing to do with the temperature in the room. "What have I done? Not my father, not his company, but me. What have I possibly done to give you such a poor opinion of me?"

"Charlie—"

"Oh, don't. I'm going to bed. You can sleep in your truck." She untucked her legs and, not giving him another look, headed to the bedroom.

She'd almost made it when a clap of thunder sounded so loudly she dropped to the floor in a crouch with her hands over her ears. Even with her eyes squeezed shut, the accompanying flash of lightning was as bright as daylight. She let out a scream, wrapping her arms over her head.

A loud crack rent the air, a tearing sound of wood splitting, followed by a crash as a tree came down so close Charlie thought she was about to be flattened. The ground shook with the impact, and she whimpered in fright. She could hardly hear the storm over the sound of heart started pounding in her ears, and she struggled to breathe evenly.

"Hey. Hey, it's alright. I've got you." Rhett's deep voice gave her something else to focus on apart from the storm.

She opened her eyes to see him crouching in front of her, his hands hovering midway between them as if uncertain if he should touch her. Another boom of thunder sounded and before she realized it, she had launched herself into his arms.

"It's going to be alright," Rhett said, tucking her head into his chest and gathering her close. "Summer storms aren't common down our way. They're usually further away in the mountains."

Being held by him shouldn't feel as good as it did. There are plenty of very good reasons to not get involved with Rhett, but as Charlie relaxed in his arms and focused on his voice, her breathing calmed, and she didn't want to be anywhere else. She slid her arms around him, and he dropped a kiss on her forehead.

"What was that noise?" She asked in a small voice.

"A tree coming down. Sounded pretty close, too."

"Oh."

"It's going to be ok, beautiful. I promise."

Despite everything, she believed him. Even with the rain smacking against the windows and the wind howling through the trees, she believed him.

Rhett settled against the wall, pulling her sideways onto his lap, his powerful arms around her. She felt worlds away from the violent storm outside.

She pulled back from where her face was buried against his chest. "Rhett?"

He reached up to smooth a stray strand of hair behind her ear. "Mmm?"

"I thought you didn't like me."

Charlie's eyes were bright, her cheeks hot as she stared up at him. This was worse than being a teenager with a crush. Her stomach was in knots.

"I like you," he said simply.

Her brows knit in confusion as she frowned.

"I like you," he said again, turning her chin gently with one finger so their eyes met. Clear blue and amber tangled. "Charlie. You are the most beautiful woman I've ever met. You're funny and determined, and I like you more than I should, considering I've known you for less than a week."

"And because of who my father is," she said.

He nodded. "And because of who your dad is, yeah."

Her memories of her childhood were of waiting up as late as her nanny would allow for her father to come home, only to fall asleep on a small chaise lounge in the entryway of their Manhattan apartment. She would see him for a brief few minutes on the weekend if she was lucky. When she had been old enough, she was sent to boarding school, spending holidays alone in the empty apartment her father barely slept in.

Sometimes she wondered what her life would have been like if her mother had lived. Charlie was barely two years old when her mother had left her with her father to marry a tech billionaire. She'd died shortly afterwards when the private jet she'd been in had crashed.

"Is that why you seem into me one minute and then ready to rip my head off the next?" She asked, a twinkle in her eye and her lips twitching.

Rhett barked out a laugh. "I'm not angry at you." He shook his head. "I'm angry at me."

"What?"

"I shouldn't want to be anywhere near you, but I can't stay away. My grandfather fought for decades to keep that land. He never wanted it sold, he was determined to keep it the way it was so people could enjoy it. He always said that you can't stop progress, but he was damned if he'd let it run him over." Rhett smiled wistfully, staring into the distance. He shook his head. "That's why, beautiful. I can't sell or I'd be going against everything he wanted."

"Oh." Charlie couldn't think of anything to say.

"He was pretty much my dad. My parents died when I was eleven and he took me in. He was with me longer than my own parents were. I can't just sell up and go against everything he stood for."

Charlie's chest squeezed in sympathy. She knew what it felt like to be caught up in the expectations of family, and she couldn't fault Rhett.

"I'm sorry," she said.

"Why? It was a long time ago." He smiled and brushed the side of her face with his thumb, his hand cupping her head gently.

"But I'm sorry for barreling into your life and bringing all that up. I can see why you don't want to sell."

"You can?"

She laughed. "Don't look so shocked. I told you I wasn't like my father."

He smiled. "You're right. You did."

She wiggled on his lap, moving to stand up. He let her go, staring up at her from his position on the floor.

"Well?" She asked, a hand on one cocked hip and a smile on her lips.

"Well, what?"

"Are you coming to bed?"

She laughed as he scrambled to his feet and followed her into the shadowy bedroom.

# Chapter Six

**Rhett**

Charlie stopped in the middle of the small room next to the bed, her hand resting on the cast-iron frame. It wasn't a large bed, barely big enough for Rhett on his own, which he knew because he'd stayed here a lot in the months after his grandfather had died. This particular cabin was as familiar to him as his own home.

Rhett padded up to her on bare feet, the air in the cabin having cooled with the storm that still raged around them, and the floorboards with it. He reached for her hand, sliding his fingers into hers and tugging her gently to face him.

"I can sleep in my truck."

"I know," she said. "But what if I get scared?"

He fought back a smile at her exaggerated pout. "We can't have that now, can we?"

She shook her head.

"I should warn you, I'm a cuddler."

This time, he laughed. "You make that sound like a threat."

She poked him in the chest with her pointer finger. "It was."

Rhett captured her hand, holding it against his chest. "That's alright. I think I can handle you."

She smirked, her eyes sparkling.

"The things I want to do to you, beautiful." He practically growled, enjoying the way her breathing got faster, and her cheeks went pink.

"Oh, really?"

Her pulse fluttered under his fingers. Rhett lifted her captured hand to his neck, and she took the cue, sliding both arms around him and rising on her toes. Her breasts pushed against his chest and Rhett groaned, the sound dragged from deep inside him.

"You're so beautiful it hurts."

Charlie's cropped tee and leggings had parted at the waist to expose soft, warm skin. Rhett's hand slipped around her waist and up her back, underneath her tee shirt, his other hands cupping the back of her head, silky soft hair falling in waves through his fingers.

She moaned at his touch, shivering under his hands. Rhett had to hold himself still for long seconds, thinking about things other than the woman in his arms making noises that had his cock turning to steel.

"You say the sweetest things, big guy."

"Big guy?" His lips twitched.

She shrugged. "If the shoe fits."

He smirked and dropped his face into the crook of her neck, breathing in her scent that was a mix of her shampoo, perfume, and something that was just purely Charlie. He couldn't get enough of her.

She whined as he trailed kisses up the side of her neck towards her mouth. She turned her head so their lips met; hers parting under his and their tongues tangling.

The relief of kissing her again rushed through him, his knees almost giving way. Her hands grabbed at his hair, pulling his head down insistently and deepening their kiss. Rhett growled, dropping his hands to her backside and lifting her up against him. Her legs opened to spread around him as he canted his hips almost desperately, thrusting against her core.

She moaned and pulled away, her head falling back. Rhett took advantage of the extra space and pushed her shirt up to expose her breasts encased temptingly in a red lace bra, her pebbled nipples visible through the fabric.

"You are a surprise," he said as he stared at her breasts. He dropped his head forward and captured one of her nipples in his mouth, nipping it with his teeth.

She writhed in his arms, grinding herself against his hard dick. It was almost too much. Rhett needed her to be closer and to have his hands freed. He turned his back to the bed and sat, pulling her onto his lap in imitation of the first night they'd met.

Lightning flashed again, creating an almost stop-motion image of Charlie as she leaned forward to free her arms from her cardigan. She tossed it carelessly into a corner of the room, her cropped tee following almost immediately.

"Hello," she said as she smiled at him.

"Hi yourself," he replied with a grin before he dropped his face to her breasts once more. Chuckling against her soft, warm skin, he trailed his lips into the valley between her breasts. The clasp on her bra proved difficult, the back closures seeming to have more hooks than he'd ever seen on a bra. Charlie laughed and helped him when he swore and scowled. She deftly released the clasp, pulling the straps down her arms and flinging the lacy garment away.

Rhett groaned and reached out to cup her breasts in his hands; his callused fingers brushing over her nipples that tightened under his touch.

"My hands aren't too rough?" he asked, conscious that the work he did didn't lend itself to soft fingers.

"No. They're perfect. You're perfect." Charlie moaned, her hands gripping his hair and pulling his head to her breasts.

Not one to miss a hint, he cupped her soft breasts in his hands and bent to soothe first one nipple, then the other with his tongue.

"Yes, keep doing that." Charlie panted.

He grinned against her skin. There was nothing for it but to oblige the lady, but first he had to get more comfortable. Releasing her breasts, he picked her up and turned to climb onto the bed properly, Charlie squeaking as he moved.

"I'm way too heavy for you to be doing that," she admonished him.

He laughed. "You're really not. I'm no lightweight, beautiful. I can carry you easily." He dropped his face between her breasts, worshipping her softness as he gently lowered her back against the quilt.

He lifted his head and kissed her, devouring her with intense open-mouthed kisses that left both of them breathless. Using one hand to hold himself up over her, he slid the other into the top of her leggings. He dropped to his side next to her on the bed to get better access, throwing a thick thigh over her leg.

Charlie moaned, her hands sliding over his chest as

she tugged at his shirt. He tore himself away with diffi-culty, tearing his shirt off and throwing it carelessly across the room. When he turned back to her, he paused, loving the way she stared at his bare chest with fiery eyes.

"Rhett, please," she panted, rubbing herself against his thigh, her hips lifting in unspoken invitation.

He slid his hand back into her leggings and into the top of her lace panties. He growled when his fingers found her soaking wet, the curls of her pubic hair damp with her desire.

"Tell me what you want, Charlie," he said as he kissed his way down the curve of her stomach. His hand paused, two fingers resting on either side of her clitoris.

She shifted her hips, and he smiled against the soft skin of her belly, nipping her gently as she arched her hips off the bed.

"Touch me, please!"

He lifted his head, grinning, a wicked look in his eyes. "I am touching you."

She scowled, and he bit his lip trying not to laugh.

"You know where."

He shrugged one shoulder and began to pull his hand from her leggings, but she gripped his wrist and held him there.

"I want you to touch me, Rhett. I want you to slide

your fingers over my pussy until I'm screaming for you. I want you to lick my clit and make me come—"

He growled, rising to his knees and grabbed her leggings, yanking them down to her ankles. She squeaked as he lifted her legs, baring her to his inspection.

"You're absolutely soaking for me." He slid a finger through her wet folds, then brought it to his mouth and licked his finger. She moaned as she watched him, her hands clenching and unclenching on the quilt. "You taste so sweet, beautiful. How am I ever going to get enough?"

Lightning flashed again, and Rhett was shocked to stillness by her beauty. Her hair was spread around her on the pillow, a silken mass of chestnut brown, and her amber eyes were hot with desire.

Rhett ducked his head between her legs, the leggings around her ankles catching him around the back of his neck and pulling him towards her.

His eyes dropped to the flushed pink core of her, and his dick twitched as he groaned.

*Get control of yourself, man!*

He paused, closing his eyes and taking some deep breaths.

"Are you ok?" Charlie asked, looking at him with concerned eyes.

He smiled, and the tension he'd been holding in his

chest since that morning eased. He was right where he wanted to be. "Yeah, just taking a moment."

She smirked. "Not second guessing sleeping in your truck?"

He mock scowled at her. "Not on your life." And dropped his hand to her wet pussy with a gentle smack.

Charlie moaned, her back arching off the bed and her breasts thrust forwards like a sensual goddess made just for him. She was blindingly beautiful, with her soft breasts and thighs. He couldn't get enough of her.

His fingers had slipped over her, spreading her wet arousal over her clit in light flicks that had her gasping. He spread her labia with his fingers, and settled more comfortably on his stomach to lick her opening with the flat of his tongue in long, languid strokes.

Charlie's fingers speared into his hair, tugging on the strands and sending sparks of pain though his scalp that only added to his arousal. He was hers and she was his. The minutes fell away as he listened to her gasps and moans, taking his time to discover what she liked.

When she was a mumbling, incoherent mess, he slid first one, then a second finger inside her, curling them towards her belly in a way that had her gasping and grinding her pussy down onto his hand, his palm firm against her clit.

He lifted his head as another flash of lightning lit the room. Watching her come apart on his fingers, he lifted his hips enough to unfasten his jeans. He shoved them down and grabbed his cock, groaning against her clit as he gripped himself and stroked.

Her walls tightened on his fingers. "That's it, beautiful. Give me everything you have. Let go," he growled as she fucked herself to orgasm onto his fingers.

Watching her come apart was all Rhett needed to follow her, his hand wrapped around his cock and hot cum spilling over his fingers.

She shivered, sliding her hand under his to keep him from touching her pussy. "Too sensitive," she gasped, flopping back against the pillows.

"I'll be right back," he said.

Rhett quickly stripped and went to the bathroom to clean himself up. He grabbed a washer and brought it back to Charlie, who took it with a smile and thanks.

"Are you okay?" he asked as he lifted the quilt for her to slip underneath.

"God yes." She laughed. "But what about you?"

"I couldn't have held back if I'd tried. I came with you," he admitted with a wink.

"What? Really?" Her eyes were wide as she stared up at him.

"Yup. The way you came apart on my tongue was too much for me, beautiful." He dropped a kiss to her temple and dragged her against his side.

She slid next to him, her breasts pushed against his bare chest. His dick twitched.

"Go to sleep," he said, equally talking to Charlie and his dick.

She curled against his side, and they both drifted off to sleep to the sound of rain on the windows.

# Chapter Seven

## Rhett

It was the early hours of the morning when Rhett woke, Charlie's warm curves curled into his side. He was lying on his back, with Charlie using his shoulder as a pillow, her hand resting on his chest. Her breath was slow and soft, relaxed in sleep.

He couldn't resist rubbing his cheek against her soft hair. The scent of her enveloped him and a deep sense of contentment had him smiling.

Surely last night was just the beginning. Even if she was only in Cape Wilde for a few days, who knew where this could lead? He may as well make the most of whatever time they had. He smiled as he took his time watching her sleep. Her eyelashes were long, swooping over cheeks dotted with fine freckles.

The sunlight broke through the trees. It was past time to get up, and he slipped out from under Charlie's arm and padded into the kitchen, a towel wrapped around his waist. While he waited for the coffee to brew, he pulled on his boots and went out to his truck, feeling more than a little silly in boots and a towel.

The cause of the noise the night before became clear. Rhett paused with a hand resting on the side of the truck. A tree had fallen across the track, completely blocking the way back to Cape Wilde. Had it fallen in a different direction, it could have hit the cabin. He shook his head. They'd been lucky. He'd have to move it before they could leave, and he didn't like the idea of Charlie out here alone without him checking to see if there were any other trees likely to come down.

All that could wait until after he'd had at least one cup of coffee.

Rhett grabbed the duffel he kept on the backseat and headed back to the cabin. Toeing off his boots, he reached inside the bag and pulled out the old pair of jeans and a tee shirt he kept in the truck. He dressed quickly and soon had coffee in hand. It wasn't anything like Joe and Pierre made at Wilde Buns, but it was passable.

His morning lifeblood restored, he was leaning with one hip propped on the cabin door, staring into the early light when Charlie approached. She was wearing a pair of pink flannel pajama pants with cartoon cats of all different colors, and the cardigan from last night wrapped tightly around her against the chill morning air.

"Good morning," she said.

Rhett grunted. Great, just the impression he wanted to make. Sophisticated man here, grunting at the polished city slicker.

"So, um. Can we talk?" she asked, her hands twisting the hem of her shirt nervously. "I have an idea."

"Sure," he said, turning to lean into the jam. He sipped his coffee as he waited for her to start.

"What if you didn't have to sell the land?"

He laughed. "I don't have to sell it."

She huffed and bit her bottom lip, staring out the door. "I know that. But it's obvious you need money."

He shifted, shoulders stiffening.

"Look," she said, her voice soft, "there's a lot of opportunity here. The land is great, the views are amazing—"

"I'm not building some resort—"

She held up a hand. "Just listen. Please."

He had a bad feeling about this, so he drained his cup and returned it to the kitchen. "Can it wait? I have to get rid of a tree blocking the trail or we'll never get out of here."

He knew he was being an asshole, but he didn't want to stand here and have her pick apart his business. He did the best he could with the resources he had. He hadn't gone to college, had barely finished high school, but he wasn't blind. He knew what she saw.

Wilde Outdoor Adventures was barely operating in this century, let alone this decade. He didn't want to spoil what he'd felt last night by having her look down on him.

He rinsed his cup out, heading towards the door to pull his boots on.

"There's a tree?"

Rhett gestured past the truck, glad that she appeared to have lost interest in talking about the land again.

"Oh, wow. That's certainly a problem." She grimaced. "Can I help?"

Rhett bent to pull his boots on and tie the laces. "No, I've done plenty of these before. It shouldn't take too long to clear enough to get past in the truck." He straightened. "I'm not sure about your rental, though."

Charlie bit her lip. "I'm stuck here?"

"No, beautiful." He dropped a kiss to her nose, smirking as she scrunched her face up. "But you can't stay here." He explained about the other trees and the risk of limbs coming down after a storm and she paled.

"I'll pack my things," she said.

He nodded, striding towards his truck to grab an axe from the trunk on the back. He paused, one hand on the latch and his breath caught at the sight of her standing in the doorway to the cabin. Her hair was messed from sleep, and she was still in pajamas, but it didn't matter to him.

She was still the most stunningly beautiful woman he'd ever seen.

Charlie lifted her hand, and he smiled, lifting his in return.

*Be cool, man. Be cool.*

He yanked the trunk open and grabbed the axe, turning to walk to where the tree fell across the track. He started by trimming the smaller branches, and it didn't take him long to work up a sweat. He pulled his shirt off, draping it over a branch and kept going, falling into the familiar rhythm of chopping wood.

It was half an hour later and the sun had risen properly when he heard Charlie calling his name. He finished dragging the limb to the side of the track and turned to see her standing a dozen or so feet away. She was holding a flask in one hand, and a plate in the other, frozen in place. Her mouth dropped open as she stared at Rhett.

He looked down at himself and then back at her. "What?"

She snapped her mouth shut and then dragged her eyes to his, her cheeks flaming red. She took a step towards him and held her hands out.

"I thought you might be hungry."

Rhett's stomach growled. "Sounds like you're right."

He was famished. He hadn't eaten since lunch the day before and swinging an axe had worked up an appetite.

He grabbed his shirt from the branch where he'd hung it and mopped the sweat from his neck and chest with it. "Thanks."

She went to speak but squeaked and then cleared her throat. "You're welcome."

"Charlie?"

She closed her eyes, still holding the plate and flask out. "Yes, Rhett?"

"Open your eyes."

Her eyes snapped open, and her brown eyes met his. Her tongue darted out to wet her bottom lip, and she chewed on it as she looked down, her eyes trailing over his still bare chest before snapping back up to his face. Her cheeks were bright red and Rhett smiled, enjoying the effect he had on her.

"Surely you've seen a man without a shirt before?"

"Of course," she scoffed. She extended her arms towards him. "Here."

Rhett ignored the food and hooked a thumb through his belt loop. "Beautiful, you have not turned beet red just from seeing me without a shirt?" Rhett chuckled as he tossed the item of clothing in question over one shoulder and moved to stand directly in front of her.

Charlie was forced to tilt her head back to meet his eyes or stare at his chest, so she just closed her eyes. Her chest rose and fell rapidly with her breathing. The breeze whipped strands of chestnut brown hair around her face and Rhett couldn't help but reach out to finger one soft lock.

"Beautiful," he said with a groan, and bent to drop a light kiss on her lips.

She moaned, kissing him back, before pulling away with a gasp. "Do you have any idea how you look right now?" She panted.

"Uh, no?" He took the flask and the plate from her, freeing her hands.

She shook her head at him. "You are all muscles and sweaty bronzed skin," she reached out with a finger and trailed it down the middle of his chest, following a drop of sweat that was trickling slowly south. "These jeans," she tugged on the waistband, "are far too large and you have no idea what these make me think of." She traced her fingers over the vee of his obliques.

Rhett's skin flamed under her touch and the jeans that she called far too large suddenly felt far too small.

She lifted an eyebrow and grinned. "Now do you understand why I'm a bit flustered?" She walked around him in a slow circle, trailing her finger over his skin as she did. "I want to climb you like a tree." She finished her circle and stood in front of him again. "But I have turned that cabin inside out and there isn't a single condom in there, so no tree climbing for me." She turned as she sang the last word, smirking at him over her shoulder as she walked away.

Rhett watched her hips sway as she left, unable to help but laugh. She was sassy, and he loved every second.

Once she was back in the cabin, he ate the food and got back to work. It didn't take him long to finish with the tree, moving enough branches to drive the truck out. He'd have to come back with his cousin Logan and a chainsaw to make the track serviceable, but for now, this would do.

Donning his shirt, he headed back to the cabin to find Charlie had cleaned up. It didn't feel right to not see any evidence of her stay here. Like last night had never happened.

Like she was never in his life.

He rubbed at the center of his chest, frowning.

Charlie emerged from the bedroom, a tote bag in hand, and placed it on a small suitcase near the door.

"Good to go?"

She nodded. "Yeah."

He went to grab her suitcase, but she batted his hand away. "I've got it."

He lifted an eyebrow. "I know, but would it hurt to let me help?"

She gave him a strange look that he couldn't decipher and pulled her hand away. "Alright."

Rhett picked up her bag and carried it to the truck. He helped Charlie inside, thankful that he'd cleaned it out only the week prior.

They had almost made it back to Cape Wilde when Charlie turned to him. "Um, where am I going to stay? It was hard enough getting the booking for your cabin at this time of year."

He shot her a look. "I assumed you'd be staying with me."

She smirked, an eyebrow raised. "That's a bit of an assumption there, big guy."

He laughed. "I'm not that big."

"Compared to me you are. I'd rather not stay with you."

He scowled. "Why not?"

"I don't want you getting any more ideas about my motivations."

Oh. That made sense, even if he would prefer it if she were with him. In his bed. In his life.

He shoved the thought deep inside and locked it down tight. She was only here for a few more days.

"So, where are you going to stay? You're right, there are no vacancies this time of year."

She grinned at him. "I'm going to stay with you."

Rhett groaned and shook his head. "I thought you just said—"

"As long as you promise not to go down that whole weird thing where you think my father sent me to prostitute myself in order to get you to sell that land."

"I never said—"

"Uh, huh."

Rhett shot her a glance and the tilt of her head, raised eyebrows and crossed arms told him everything he needed to know. "Yeah, ok. I won't."

"Promise?"

"I promise."

She giggled. "And you'd better make sure you have some condoms, because there's no way I'm staying under the same roof as you again without riding that gorgeous cock of yours."

Rhett choked, coughing and laughing at the same time.

"Yes, ma'am."

# Chapter Eight

## Charlie

Rhett's house turned out to be barely more than a cabin itself. A two-bedroom wooden home on the outskirts of the town, facing the water. He parked and helped Charlie out of the truck, carrying her suit-case inside. When he ducked back out to get his own gear, she took the opportunity to look around. The living room looked over the marina and the ocean in the far distance. There was no television, just a faded sofa and a bookshelf stuffed to overflowing with well-thumbed paperbacks. The kitchen was a small but practical space, with worn but clean and serviceable cabinetry and mismatched appliances, and that's where Rhett found her when he came back inside.

"It's a nice view, isn't it?" He said, standing next to her, nodding towards the living room.

"Yeah."

"You never got around to telling me your idea." He turned to lean against the sink. Rhett reached out and put his hands on her hips, his large fingers splayed across her back, thumbs pressing gently into the softness of her belly.

She'd never been around people who were so casually tactile as Rhett, and she decided she liked it. Charlie stepped between his legs and rested her hands on his shoulders, brushing her own thumbs up and down his neck.

"Are you sure you want to hear it? It's about the land," she said, but continued in a rush, "but I promise it's not about selling it."

He nodded. "Okay. I'm listening."

"So I spoke with my father's 2IC today about the land and the deal they were offering."

Rhett's fingers twitched on her side, the only indication of his mood. He nodded for her to continue.

"You're not opposed to all development, are you? Just something as large as the resort that Sinclair Properties is proposing."

"That's right. I'd planned on renovating the cabins at some point—maybe adding a few more—but just don't have the money to spare."

She nodded. It was clear there wasn't money in the business. And he wasn't spending it anywhere else. His truck was in good condition, but it wasn't the latest model, and his house was spartan. He didn't even own a TV.

Rhett West might be many things, but he wasn't a rich man. And it was clear he wasn't motivated by money because he could have taken any of the offers her father had made over the years, but he didn't.

He was not a gold digger.

Something settled inside Charlie. A certainty that she'd found someone that she really connected with, rather than someone who had connected with what her money could do for them.

"So, you're not opposed to updating the cabins and possibly adding some more?"

"Sure, but did you hear the part where I said I didn't have the money?" He huffed out a laugh. "It's a dream, Charlie. Not reality."

She smiled up at him, her hands going around his neck. "What if it could be?"

"What are you talking about?"

"When I went to college, my father wanted me to go on to law school, so I did."

"You're a lawyer?" Rhett's mouth dropped open.

Oh no, she wasn't going to have any of that. "Yes, but I don't practice. As long as I studied what he wanted, I could take whatever extra courses I wanted."

"Sounds like a good deal."

"It was," she laughed. "I stumbled across some geography courses and loved them. One in particular about ecotourism."

Rhett lifted his eyebrows.

"What if you didn't have to sell? What if you had a partner instead who could provide the cash that you need to do the renovations on the cabins and build a small lodge? Somewhere you could use for the tours and accommodation for those who aren't able to camp or don't want to camp."

"I wouldn't own it though, would I?" He asked.

She smiled, pleased he was at least asking questions and not dismissing her outright. "There'd be paperwork to sort out, of course."

"Lawyers."

"Hey," she swiped at his chest with her hand. "I'm a lawyer."

"You said you weren't practicing."

She grumbled at him, but only in jest. "We could negotiate the ownership. Say, 51% to you and—"

"No, more than that."

She laughed. "We can talk."

"Alright, we'll talk about it," he said.

She squealed with excitement and rose on her toes to kiss him.

He laughed, setting her away from him slightly. "But not right now. I have to go to work. Will you be all right by yourself?"

"Of course. Don't worry about me. I'll write up the proposal for you."

Rhett nodded. "Sixty forty."

Charlie shook her head. "You drive a hard bargain, Rhett West."

# Chapter Nine

**Rhett**

He'd barely made it back to the shop when a family of six walked in to hire gear for a camping trip. Their own had been destroyed in the storm, but they were determined to make the most of the rest of their vacation.

Rhett helped them make their selections and no sooner had they left than the phone rang. On it went, racing from one customer to the next. Taking bookings, sorting out hired gear that had been returned and needed checking and packing before being stored away, ready for the next rental.

By the time he was ready to turn the sign on the door to 'closed' it was approaching sunset and Rhett was exhausted, so he wasn't particularly pleased to hear the bell jangle over the front door again.

He sighed, running his hand through his hair and forcing a smile on his face that he really didn't feel. He just wanted to go home to Charlie. His heart kicked at the thought, a genuine smile lifting his lips.

When Rhett entered the front room, it was to see a man in a slightly rumpled suit running his finger over a table to inspect for dust. There was something about him that put Rhett on edge, so there was no hint of a smile in his voice when he greeted the newcomer.

"Can I help you?" He asked, habit forcing him to be polite.

The other man turned and smiled, his teeth far too white and even, his blond hair slicked back, not a strand out of place.

"Rhett West?"

"The same." What did this guy want?

The man walked towards Rhett and held out his hand. Rhett gripped it automatically, not at all surprised when his hand was squeezed a little too hard for politeness.

"Prescott St Johns," he said with a smile, as if expecting Rhett to know who he was.

Rhett looked down at Prescott, and squeezed his hand in return. Prescott's face went a little pale before extracting his now slightly wrung hand.

"Can I help you?" Rhett repeated.

Prescott cleared his throat. He tuned his head and gestured to the front room. "It's more like, can I help you?" His smile was far too wide to be authentic, a show of friendliness that reminded Rhett of a salesman with a limited time deal. There was something about the guy, like a child playing at being an adult. He couldn't be over thirty years old, but the suit gave the impression he was older, and Rhett would bet that's exactly why Prescott was wearing it.

"Whatever it is you're selling, I'm not buying."

Prescott laughed, but when Rhett didn't join in, he stopped. "I'm not selling anything. I'm here to buy. I'm from Sinclair Properties and we have an offer—"

Rhett sighed. "Not interested."

"It's an incredible offer." He said, emphasizing the word incredible in a way that set Rhett's teeth on edge.

"Still not interested."

Prescott dropped all pretense of friendliness. "It's for twice what the last offer was for. How much do you need to clean up this dump, huh?" He stared around the room, oblivious to the glower Rhett was delivering him. "It's obvious you can't afford to fix the place. Face it, you're in over your head."

Rhett's hands were in such tight fists his knuckles began to ache. He took a step towards Prescott. "You drove all the way from New York to tell me that? What made you think that this time I'd accept the offer?"

"Oh, I was already in the area. Mr. Sinclair asked me to pop by to pick up his daughter, considering how close we are."

"You're friends with Charlie?" Jealousy flared to life at the thought of Charlie and this peacock being in any way more than friends. He fought to calm his breathing. Whatever she did before didn't matter. Whoever she did it with didn't matter either.

Prescott smiled like a cat who'd got the cream. "Oh, I wouldn't say we're just friends. Charlotte and I go way back." He emphasized her name, picking an imaginary piece of lint from his suit jacket. He brushed his hand down the fabric with a frown. "Actually, I suppose I may as well give you a word of warning."

Rhett didn't trust this man as far as he could throw him, but the earlier doubt he had about Charlie and her motives roared to life like gas on a smoldering fire. "About what?"

"She'll say whatever she needs to get you to sign. Do whatever she needs to. Her father has given her a challenge to prove herself. If she doesn't get you to sell, she's out. She doesn't even have the authority to make a deal. She needs Mr. Sinclair to approve it, which he has not."

That couldn't be true. She would have said something, wouldn't she?

Rhett barely heard Prescott as he left, the bell jangling in his wake. He locked up on autopilot and headed home.

He had to talk to Charlie. Now.

# Chapter Ten

## Charlie

While Rhett had gone to work, Charlie had undertaken what she had thought would be a simple task of getting a new rental. It turned out the sole rental company in the area was completely booked out. They'd given her a list of the closest alternatives and she'd spent the afternoon leaving messages and taking calls. She hung up the phone after the fourth—and final—rental company told her they couldn't get a car to her in Cape Wilde for at least another two days.

The cell phone buzzed on the kitchen counter, almost tumbling off and onto the floor before she caught it. Maybe there had been a cancellation and there was a car for her after all?

"Hello?"

"Charlotte, I'm here to take you home."

What was Prescott doing in Cape Wilde? Her father surely hadn't sent him all this way just to collect her? She pulled the phone away from her ear and stared at it in confusion.

"Did you come all this way just to do that?"

He laughed, the sound twisting her stomach. "Oh no. I was nearby and offered."

"Out of the kindness of your heart, I suppose," she muttered, not believing a second of it. "I have work to do here, so you'll just have to go back without me."

"Work? On that pathetic little joint venture idea? Why did you think it had been approved?"

What? She'd spoken to her father's 2IC herself, which was normally as good as speaking to her father, and he'd promised to call her if there was anything to clarify. She'd thought they'd trusted her finally. What was going on? Something wasn't right.

She felt sick. What would Rhett say? She'd all but promised him—no. She had to sort this out. "Prescott, what exactly did my father say?"

She could hear the smile in his voice, and narrowed her eyes. Regrettably, she'd dated Prescott briefly during college. They'd both been studying law, and he'd been attentive to her, taking her out to dinner and listening when she spoke. To her shame, it had taken her six months to realize all he wanted was to get closer to her father. Prescott hadn't loved her. He'd loved the idea of her and everything she represented.

Besides, his name wasn't even Prescott. It was Paul. He was as fake as the Rolex he wore in college. She shuddered. She'd considered him a bullet dodged, until he'd wormed his way into Sinclair Properties.

"He wants you to return to discuss this in more detail."

Prescott was a scheming ladder climber. She didn't trust him, but there was too much at stake to dismiss what he said.

"Really? Why didn't he just call me himself?" Her brow wrinkled.

"Oh, you know what he's like."

She did, and far better than Prescott, but she let him talk.

"Happy to let you have your fun, but the final decision always goes to him. Hmm?"

He wasn't wrong. She shifted from foot to foot. She didn't want to go back to New York, least of all with Prescott, but with her car stuck behind a felled tree and no rental available, she had little choice.

Oh goodie.

She told Prescott where to meet her and hung up, dropping her phone to the counter and staring off into space. Her stomach twisted, and she winced as she imaged what Rhett would think about her leaving so quickly.

He'd understand, wouldn't he? She chewed on her bottom lip. They hardly knew each other. Would he trust her? He had plenty of reason not to, but she'd just have to make him listen.

The sound of Rhett's truck pulling up alongside the house had her pulse quickening. The rumble of the engine quietened, his booted feet on the steps to the front porch seeming to echo in the quiet house. She turned to face the front door, twisting the hem of her tee shirt in her hands.

Rhett stepped into the house, not bothering to take off his boots.

"Rhett? Oh good, you're home. I—"

"You need to leave."

His words landed like bombs, her chest constricting as she blinked at him in confusion.

"What?"

He paced slowly towards her. "I should have known this would happen."

"What would happen? Rhett, you're not making any sense."

"No, what doesn't make any sense is why Sinclair's beautiful daughter would want to move to a small town like Cape Wilde and go into a partnership with me."

She paled. "Rhett, I told you—"

He kept talking, not paying attention to her. His mind was already made up. "How many college degrees do you have, Charlie? Or should I call you Charlotte, like Prescott does?"

Oh. Well, that explained things a little better. Not only was her ex here, but he'd taken the time to stick his nose into her business.

"Why?" She faced him down, her arms crossed over her chest. "Are you judging me now? Why does my education matter?"

He snorted. "I knew you were too good for me."

Too good for him? What did that mean? What exactly had Prescott told Rhett?

"What? That's a load of crap and you know it, Rhett West." She was angry now. Furious at him for his lack of trust. For not coming to speak with her first before believing the bullshit the likes of Prescott St Johns would spread like fertilizer.

"Is it, though? Can you tell me with certainty that your proposal has the support of your father?"

Charlie pressed her lips together and didn't answer. She couldn't tell him that. At least not right now.

Rhett turned away, hands on his hips, walking a few paces before turning on her. He scoffed. "See? I knew it. It was all a lie."

"You want to believe that, don't you?" She whispered. Her heart felt like it was shattering into pieces. Was he that convinced that he was unlovable? That nobody—no woman—would ever want what he could offer?

"Who hurt you so badly that you're willing to push me away at the first hint of a problem?"

He winced as if she'd struck him and she had the satisfaction of knowing she was right. It wasn't a good feeling at all. She hated that this was happening. Hated that she would have to leave to sort this out, and that leaving was exactly what he expected her to do.

"I'll leave, but I'm coming back. And you're going to sit down and talk this through with me, Rhett West."

He crossed his arms and ignored her, staring over her head.

A car horn beeped outside.

"That will be your... what exactly is he to you, Charlie?" Rhett almost spat the words.

"He's nothing."

"Didn't sound like it to me," he replied, watching her as she stuffed her laptop and charger into her tote.

She hadn't even unpacked her suitcase, so she simply grabbed it from where she had left it against the wall, extending the handle with a decisive snap. She slung her tote over her shoulder and took one last look at Rhett.

"I thought you would believe me over someone you

don't know," she said, shaking her head. She fought back tears with rapid blinks, not wanting to cry in front of Rhett or Prescott.

"Yeah, well, I thought I knew you. Turns out I was wrong."

The words stung like a whip, the tears fell, and she walked out the door.

# Chapter Eleven

**Rhett**

The good thing about it being the summer was that Rhett could work himself half to death to avoid thinking about Charlie with little trouble. One week turned into two, which turned into three, and the ache in his chest didn't ease one bit.

He knew he was avoiding his family. He wasn't answering Cassie's calls, and hadn't turned up for the weekly family dinner with his cousins and his aunt for over a month, using the excuse that the season was busy and he needed to work.

And he hadn't heard a peep from Charlie.

In the first week, he thought he'd at least get a text from her to apologize. Then in the second, possibly an email. He was ashamed of the number of times he'd sat on his porch staring out across the marina, a beer in one hand and his phone in the other, thumb hovering over the 'call' button.

But he hadn't called.

He had looked her up online and seen her smiling face in a corporate headshot, looking so polished and perfect that he'd known he was right. He was nowhere near good enough for her. He hadn't looked again.

What had she seen in him? He was just a small-town guy with a rundown business and no education.

It was late one afternoon towards the end of the summer when Rhett pulled up at the back of the shop. His cousin Logan had offered to look after the shop for the day while Rhett took a group hiking, and was waiting when Rhett returned.

"About time you got back," Logan grumbled. He grabbed his keys out of his pocket and jiggled them impatiently as he stood next to the storage shed at the back of the building.

Rhett ignored his cousin as he let down the truck's tailgate to unpack the gear. Logan stuffed his keys back in his pocket with a sigh and came to help. He might have the reputation for being a bit of a loner, but would always pitch in to help his family. As long as he didn't have to deal with too many people, he was happy.

The two men worked in silence like only those who have worked together for a long time can. They'd just grabbed the last of the gear from Rhett's truck when he stopped and turned to Logan.

"Can I ask you something?"

Logan paused, hands tucked into his belt. "Sure."

"Do you ever get lonely?"

Logan frowned, dropping his head down so the brim of his tattered ball cap obscured his face. "Yes... and no."

"Care to explain?"

Logan grabbed the last box as Rhett packed away the straps and folded up the tailgate. Rhett knew not to push his cousin. A man of few words, he'd answer when he was ready and not a moment earlier. It was a trait Rhett usually appreciated, but right now, he was impatient.

Logan returned from putting the trunk away and pulled the door of the storage shed shut. His booted feet scuffed the worn concrete as he ambled back to Rhett.

"I like my life," he drawled. "I had plenty of busy before..." he shrugged, a half smile on his face briefly before his face settled into its habitual scowl.

It had been such a long time ago that Rhett often forgot that Logan went to college on a football scholarship. That he'd even made the draft... and then given it all up to come back to Cape Wilde before even seeing a single NFL game. All because his family needed him.

If Logan wanted more from life, he'd go chase it.

"I like my life," Logan said again. "I enjoy living in a place where I know what to expect. Where the seasons mean change but of a predictable type. I like living where I do." He jerked his head towards the road out of town where the house he had painstakingly renovated over the past two years was on a wooded rise overlooking the ocean.

"I like my job. I love my family."

Rhett nodded, and the two leaned against the truck. He tilted his head back, watching as a seabird circled overhead on the air currents, looking for its next meal. Rhett envied its simple life and its freedom.

"So you never get lonely."

"I didn't say that," Logan smiled a rare smile. "I like a woman's company. I've dated a time or two."

Rhett's mouth dropped open. "Who? When? How come this is the first I'm hearing about it?"

Logan barked out a laugh, clearly enjoying surprising his younger cousin. "I'm not someone who enjoys people knowing his business."

"Yeah, I know," Rhett mumbled, a bit embarrassed for having started the conversation.

"You started this conversation." Logan elbowed him in jest.

"Are you a mind reader now?"

He smiled again and cuffed Rhett on the shoulder.

"When someone asks a question like that, it's usually because they want someone to ask them the same thing." He shot Rhett a pointed look. "You in love with Charlie?"

Rhett choked, and Logan slapped him on the back.

"Ah well, never mind. You'll see her soon enough, I bet."

That stopped Rhett. "What?"

Logan gave his cousin a pitying look. "You're not stupid, Rhett. You've been moping around for the last month. Before that, you were the happiest I'd ever seen you. All you could talk about was Charlie this and Charlie that." He lifted an eyebrow. "It was kind of sickening, to be honest."

Rhett pulled a face. "What do I do?"

"You make it up to her, idiot."

"You just said I wasn't stupid!"

Logan snorted. "So don't act like it. If you love her, get her back."

Rhett suddenly felt like he ate rocks for breakfast. "Oh."

Logan pulled his keys from his pocket and swung them around his finger. He patted Rhett on the back with one meaty hand, sending his cousin forward.

"You just going to just mope around here hoping she gets some kind of telepathic message about how you feel?" He asked, lifting one eyebrow.

"Ouch." Rhett winced.

"You asked, buddy. And someone needed to give it to you straight." He shrugged and ambled over to his truck. He climbed into the driver's seat and started it. Before he pulled away, he stopped and leaned out the window.

"Rhett?"

He turned to look at his cousin. "Yeah?"

"Sure I'm lonely. I want a family one day. But I haven't met a woman who wants me and all this." He waved his hand out the window, gesturing at the town. "They're fine with me, but they want to live in a city. And as soon as they see my place, they run for the hills." He smiled, but it was a sad smile. "I'll give you some advice, cousin of mine."

"Oh?" This should be good.

"Regrets eat at you like cancer. If you love her, show her every day."

Rhett groaned, and Logan laughed at him before driving off.

# Chapter Twelve

## Charlie

After a month of working long days that went well into the night, Charlie was ready to sleep for a week. She just needed to get through this last meeting with her father and then she could go home. 'Thank god it's Friday' had never felt more appropriate.

Charlie paused outside the door to her father's office to smooth her hair. The door was open slightly, voices drifting out. She waited, her father obviously still talking with someone. She didn't listen to what they were saying until she heard something that grabbed her attention like a nail to a magnet.

"...Rhett West is a stubborn bastard."

That was Prescott's voice. What was he saying about Rhett?

She leaned forward, moving as close as she dared and listened.

"Like his grandfather, I take it?"

"Yes, sir."

Charlie scowled.

"So he turned down the latest offer?"

The latest offer? Charlie's lips pursed. Had someone been to Cape Wilde since she had come back? She had heard nothing about that, and she'd met with her father every week to talk through her proposal. Not that he'd shown much interest, but she wasn't losing faith that he'd come around at some point. It was taking longer than she'd like, but she was determined.

"Yes, he took one look at me yesterday and told me to—ahem, well. He told me to 'fuck right off and not come back' were his exact words, sir."

Yesterday? Prescott was in Cape Wilde yesterday? Her brows drew together in confusion, even while her lips twitched at the image of the pretentious Prescott being told off in no uncertain terms by Rhett. The two were as different as oil and water.

"And what about Charlotte's proposal? Did he mention anything about that?"

Prescott laughed, and Charlie fought to not barge into the office.

"The one where we go in partnership with West?" Prescott laughed, her father joining him.

"Yes, that one. I don't know what she was thinking. Why would we want to partner with some small town hick who can't even keep his business afloat?"

Charlie clenched her teeth so hard her jaw started to cramp. How dare they speak about Rhett like that?

"All we need is a little more leverage and he'll have no choice but to sell," her father said.

Leverage? Charlie leaned a hand on the door, trying to get closer.

Prescott laughed. "Who would have thought he would have been interested in Charlotte?"

"Indeed," her father said, but this time he wasn't laughing. "No daughter of mine will be involved with someone like him. She has some silly ideas, but that cannot happen. The Sinclair name will not be dragged into the mud. Make sure of it, and that promotion will be yours."

Charlie gasped, her hand jerking where it rested on the door. The slight movement enough to push the door fully open. Her father and Prescott turned to face her.

"Oh, Charlotte. There you are. I'll be with you in a

minute." Her father turned back to Prescott as if he hadn't just been plotting to ruin her life.

"How could you?"

He stopped and sighed, turning to face her. "How could I what? Ensure your future? Ensure the future of this company? Easily, my dear. Very easily."

She backed away, shaking her head. "You're unbelievable."

Her father scoffed. "How deluded. What kind of future would you have living in a hovel with that—"

Charlie wouldn't listen to another word. "He's ten times the man you will ever be."

Prescott opened his mouth and Charlie rounded on him. "Oh, and shut the fuck up, you absolute butt-kissing fool. Can't you see he's using you to do his dirty work, *Paul*?" She sneered his name, and he spluttered.

Charlie ignored him and turned on her heel to leave.

"Where do you think you're going?"

She stopped in the doorway at her father's words, resting a hand on the frame and turning her head to glare at him. "I have enough PTO to cover my notice period. I quit."

It took far longer than Charlie expected to pack up her life in New York. When she'd finally tied up the last loose end, it was a week after she'd handed in her notice. She'd gotten into the habit of leaving her phone in her handbag, her father's PA called her at least three times a day and there was no way she was taking *that* call. She took it out, expecting to see missed calls from the familiar number.

But there it was, just like she'd hoped. A message from Rhett.

She was standing in the foyer of her bank . Uncaring of where she was, her fingers had trembled as she'd held the phone. She'd played the message through three times; she was just so happy to hear his voice.

"Charlie... uh, I'd hoped to talk to you... I'm really sorry," he'd said, his tone anguished. "I miss you so much. You're right, you know." At that point he laughed, a little self deprecatingly. "I was pushing you away. I did push you away."

There was a pause, and as Charlie listened a tear slid down her cheek. She sniffed, wiping it away with the back of her fingers, torn between happiness that Rhett had reached out and pure anxiety over why.

"I want to be with you. I need you. Charlie, all I want is for you to be happy." He drew in a ragged breath. "I know I don't deserve a second chance, but do you think you could give me one, anyway?" He laughed sadly. "Please call me back."

Charlie sank down on the cold marble of the bank's floor and sobbed.

And then she called him back.

# Chapter Thirteen

**Rhett**

Summer passed into fall, and with the changing of the seasons came the changing of Wilde Outdoor Adventures' clients. Fewer families on camping trips with their kids, and more older couples looking to catch sight of Maine's famous fall colors.

The morning sun reflected off the water as Rhett stepped out of the shop and slipped on his sunglasses. It looked like any other morning, but he felt with every part of his being that today was going to change his life.

Today he'd see Charlie again.

Today he'd make it all up to her... if she let him.

He took a deep breath of the salty air to steady his nerves and headed down the street in search of caffeine. His cousins liked to joke that he was a bear without his morning brew, but they were all just as bad.

He had just reached Wilde Buns when he saw the elderly Mrs. Trombley cross the road towards him. Her white hair was streaked with bright pink and purple, contrasting with the huge green reading glasses that were perched on her head when not being worn. She might be in her eighties, but she was one of the fittest people Rhett knew, riding her bicycle everywhere she went. She taught yoga and belly dancing at the town's community center and did tarot readings from the shop she ran in town, where she sold crystals and locally made candles.

"Morning, Mrs. Trombley," he said. "Everything all set for today?" He opened the bakery door for her.

Her eyes twinkled. "Of course. Anything for love," she laughed, patting him on the shoulder as she stepped inside. "I know she'll be good for you. I saw it in the cards. It's not right for such a fine specimen of manhood to be all alone," she said, before turning to survey the baked goods in the glass display cabinet.

He met the eyes of Joe, who co-owned Wilde Buns with his husband Pierre, both of them trying not to laugh at her description of Rhett. "Hey Rhett. What can I get you?"

"Coffee and one of those," he pointed at a savory pastry in the cabinet.

"No problem."

While he waited for his order, Rhett stared out the window. For days he'd been making plans, putting things in place, calling in favors owed and gaining new ones. All for today. If his gamble didn't pay off, then he didn't know what he'd do, but at least he could say he'd laid it all on the line.

"Here you are, Rhett," Joe said, sliding a large to-go coffee cup and a paper bag across the counter.

With a nod and a wave of thanks, Rhett headed over to the table where Logan was already sitting. Leg jiggling with nerves, he took a sip of the hot coffee and sighed.

Cassie joined them a few minutes later, bringing her own coffee and pastry to chatter with Logan—her brother— about a litter of puppies she'd delivered earlier that morning. Slowly, the tables around Rhett filled until everyone had assembled.

"Alright everyone, thank you for coming," Rhett said, standing to get their attention. He rubbed his hand over the back of his neck and chuckled. "This is not something I've ever done before—"

"I should hope not," muttered Mrs. Trombley.

Rhett ignored her. "—So I really appreciate the help." He looked around at his neighbors, friends, and family. For a long time he'd felt a little like an inter-loper in Cape Wilde, being adopted into the town but never part of it. Somewhere along the way that had changed, and all these people had volunteered to help him.

With their help, he'd show Charlie just how much he loved her, how much he loved this town, and how much he wanted her to stay.

A chorus of voices greeted him, and Rhett lifted a hand to be heard. "Alright, so let's get started." He pulled a folded piece of paper from his pocket and ran his finger down the list.

"Mrs. Trombley, you're up first."

"Card reading and tea and scones," she replied. "This is going to be so much fun!"

Rhett smiled. "Cassie?"

"Puppies are go!" There were a few chuckles at that.

"Good."

And so it went, one after another, the people of Cape Wilde went over their role in Charlie's treasure hunt. Until there was only one left.

"And finally me," he said, smiling. He folded the paper up and put it in his pocket once more.

Hopefully, this would be a day Charlie remembered for all the right reasons.

# Chapter Fourteen

## Charlie

The morning Charlie arrived in Cape Wilde for the second time was cool, but sunny. She drove straight to Wilde Outdoor Adventures, surprised to find the doors locked and nobody there. On the front door a single red rose was taped with a note.

Charlie looked around, but there was nobody about to ask. Fingers shaking, she reached for the note. Turning it over, she saw her name printed in a bold, masculine print.

*Rhett's handwriting.*

She smiled, smoothing her hand over the paper before opening the note.

*I've left you clues around the town, but not to turn*

*it upside down. Your first stop is here, as I knew it would be, the second is to Mrs. Trombley for some tea.*

Charlie laughed, delighted, and took the rose back to her car.

She had tea with Mrs. Trombley and had her fortune read, then she was taken on a brief tour of the harbor with Rhett's artist cousin, Rowan, who Rhett had described once or twice as half-fish. She moved from location to location around the town, taking in the people and places that were so special to Rhett. She saw how it was a part of him, and how it could be a part of her too. By the middle of the afternoon she'd accumulated almost a dozen red roses.

"Eleven," Charlie said as Cassie handed her one more with a smile. "Who do I get number twelve from?"

"Can you guess?" Cassie asked, holding out the final clue.

"Rhett," she said, taking the note. She opened the paper and read it with a laugh.

*The final stop is just for you and me, you'll find me waiting near THAT tree.*

Charlie laughed and, throwing a hasty thank you over her shoulder, headed out the door.

Of course he'd bring her back to the cabin where they'd been stuck in the storm. Somewhere quiet and amongst the trees he loved so much.

It didn't take her long to reach her destination. She pulled up next to where Rhett had parked his truck and turned off the engine. She bundled up her roses and climbed out of the car, walking slowly to the front door.

Her hand hesitated, unsure if she should knock or just open the door.

"Charlie," Rhett said from behind her.

She squeaked and spun on her heel to face him, holding one hand against her chest. How such a giant of a man could be so light on his feet was a mystery.

"Sorry, I didn't mean to scare you." He ran his hand over the back of his neck.

His proximity, the smell of whatever he used to launder his clothes, his deodorant and a slight whiff of wood smoke had her head spinning. It was just uniquely him. No cologne. She couldn't imagine him fussing with his appearance, and yet he looked like he'd stepped out of a designer clothes fashion shoot with the mood board of 'sexy outdoorsman'.

Jeans that looked like they were made just for him were stretched over his muscular thighs, his feet encased in heavy boots that had seen better days. He was wearing another tight tee shirt—this time black— under a plaid green and black shirt. The man seemed incapable of spending five minutes with his hair not flopping over his forehead, the brown locks just begging to be pushed back from his eyes.

He belonged here like a fish belonged in the ocean. And she loved him with every part of her.

"You got the flowers." He said. "I hope you had a good day."

She smiled and walked a step towards him, holding the roses against her chest. "Yes, they're beautiful. But isn't there meant to be one more?"

"Oh, yeah there is. Come inside." He stepped around her and pushed open the door, holding it so she could enter.

She gasped, staring around the cabin. "What have you done to this place?"

"You don't like it?"

"No! I love it!" Charlie walked into the center of the room and turned on the spot, taking it all in. The kitchen had been renovated, and the walls painted white with pale green trim. The old furniture was gone, replaced with a cozy looking sofa and a small dining table and two chairs. Brightly colored rugs adorned the floor, giving the room a bright, cheery feeling.

Charlie walked to the bathroom, Rhett following with a smile. She gasped at the claw-footed tub and the separate shower, a far cry from the old bathroom fittings. And then there was the bedroom. Floor-length gauze curtains covered the windows, and the walls were freshly painted white. An armchair and bookshelf in the corner made for a cozy reading nook, and the bed itself was covered in a handmade quilt, another bright rug on the floor.

"You did all this?" She asked, turning to face Rhett.

"I wanted you to see what it could be like," he said, flushing slightly.

"But you didn't have any money..."

Rhett nodded. "I called in some favors."

Charlie smiled. "I love it."

"You do?"

"Yes." She nodded.

"The rose," Rhett said suddenly, leaving the room.

Charlie followed him into the kitchen where a single rose sat in a vase filled with water. She put the rest of the roses in the vase and arranged them to give her hands something to do, then placed the vase in the middle of the dining table.

"So, still only one bed?" She said with a small smile.

Rhett cleared his throat. "I figured I'd go home. Unless..."

"Unless I wanted you to stay?"

"Something like that."

She turned and leaned her hip against the kitchen counter, fiddling with the hem of her sweater. "Rhett, I thought I belonged in New York. I'd been trying to fit in there for so long I didn't know what I wanted anymore. And then I met you, and I started to believe I could have a different life. One that wasn't about appearances and boardrooms, but about actually connecting with people. One filled with love."

Rhett took a step towards her, his voice rough when he spoke. "Do you still believe you can have that life?"

"Yes." She closed the distance between them and rested her hands on his chest, tilting her head back to meet his eyes. "Yes, I want that life. With you."

Rhett's smile lit his entire face. "You mean that?"

She laughed, tears in her eyes. "Rhett, I love you. I belong with you."

He gathered her into his arms and swung her around as they both laughed. She looked up at him, her cheeks hot and her eyes filled with happy tears. He set her down and rested his hands on either side of her face.

"Charlotte Sinclair. Charlie. I adore you. You are an amazing woman. You're strong, caring, kind, and compassionate. I am so sorry I didn't listen to you at first. I was afraid of getting hurt, so I pushed you away. I hurt you before you could hurt me, and it all backfired on me, anyway." He smiled sadly. "I'm sorry for not listening to you. You've given me every reason to trust you. I should have listened."

Her eyes were wet as she smiled up at him.

"I love you, Charlie. More than anything else in the world. And if that means coming with you to New York, then I will."

She gasped. "But what about the business? What about your family?"

He shrugged. "It's just a business. I love it here, yes. I've lived here almost my whole life. Sure, my family is here. But I can always visit."

He swiped his thumb over her cheek to catch a tear.

"Oh, Rhett, that means a lot to me," Charlotte said as she smiled through her tears. "But I'm staying here. I don't belong in New York anymore. I belong here, in Cape Wilde, with you."

"Are you sure?" He asked. "It's very different to New York."

"I'm sure," she said, smiling up at Rhett.

He bent down and touched his lips to hers. It was as if they'd never been apart. Heat bloomed between them as she opened to him. She slid her hand underneath his tee shirt and he growled, his hands dropping to grip her backside and lift her against him.

"I need you now, beautiful."

# Chapter Fifteen

## Charlie

There was something incredibly satisfying to the ego about having the sexiest man she had ever laid eyes on be desperate to get her naked. They were both panting as he carried her into the bedroom. The dappled sunlight streamed through the gauzy curtains and over the bed. Rhett carried her to the foot of the bed and lowered her to her feet.

His hands were urgent as he undressed her. Each slide of fabric across her skin felt like a caress, and by the time she stood before him in only her underwear, she was flushed with need.

"You too," she said, and his eyes grew hot.

He stripped in what must have been record time, tossing his clothes into a pile on the floor to stand in front of her in only his boxer briefs. He could put an underwear model to shame with those rigid abdominals and bulging biceps. She wasn't sure where to look; every part of him was stunning. He called her beautiful, but so was he. He was overwhelming in the small space of the bedroom, and she shivered.

His muscled shoulders were broad, his pecs wide and firm. She reached up and ran her fingers over his chest, marveling at how soft his skin was. Like silk over steel, the hard muscles underneath bunched at her touch, and she reveled in the thought that he was as hungry for her touch as she was for his.

She glanced down and noticed he was definitely affected, judging by the bulge in his underwear. She stifled a giggle, and he swatted her gently on her ass.

"Laughing at a man in his underwear, hmm?" he said, but there was no anger in his voice, and his eyes were warm. He pulled his boxer briefs down in one swift motion and kicked them off, his cock bobbing against his stomach.

Her laughter stopped as he reached down and stroked himself lazily with one big hand. She made a noise that was something between a squeak and a moan, and it was definitely not sexy. At all.

In an attempt to regain some ground, she reached behind her back and unclipped her bra, pulling the cups away from her chest and tossing it into the corner with his briefs. She ran her hands up her sides and cupped her heavy breasts in her hands, rubbing her nipples with her fingers and smirking as Rhett froze mid-stroke, his eyes focused on her hands as she trailed them over her body.

*Turnabout is fair play.*

Now it was Rhett's turn to groan, the sound shooting straight to her core. She bit her lip and squeezed her legs together, feeling heat rush to her center. She had never been so turned on in all her life. She was slippery between her legs and became even more so as Rhett let go of his cock and lifted his hands to her chest.

He stopped just shy of covering her. "May I?"

She nodded, and he pulled his hands away a little.

"Say it, beautiful. I need to hear that you're as into this as I am. Because if you're not, we stop. End of story. It's only good for me if it's good for you, Charlie."

She met his eyes. "Rhett, I need you to touch me. Make love to me, please?"

He closed his eyes and groaned, then dropped his lips to hers. Her head swam as he devoured her, his tongue seeking hers as one of his hands slid around her waist to palm one ass cheek and pull her hard up against him. His hard length was sandwiched between them, and she felt him throb with need. Her hands rested on his chest, her breasts brushing against him, her nipples hard.

He walked her backward until the back of her knees hit the mattress, and she fell with a squeak. He followed her down and, with quick movements, had her underneath him on the bed. One forearm rested above her head, keeping his weight off her, and he rested one big muscular thigh between her very eagerly open legs.

This was where she had wanted to be for so long she could hardly believe it was happening.

Rhett loomed over her, but she felt safe in his arms. She knew he would protect her always.

Something in her face must have shown her mood as he paused, brows furrowing. "Did I hurt you?" He started looking over her body and not in the way she was hoping.

"I'm fine, Rhett."

He shot her a look that said he didn't believe her.

"Really." She smiled, and he relaxed. "Do you want me to show you just how fine I am?"

He grinned and lowered his head to drop a kiss on her nose. "No, beautiful. You stay right where you are. Let me take care of you." His voice was deep and growly as he lowered his head to press a kiss to the side of her neck, his stubble brushing lightly against her skin and sending shivers to the tips of her toes.

She relaxed and enjoyed the sensation as he trailed kisses across her collarbone, working his way to the center of her chest, before dropping his head to capture one of her nipples between his teeth. He nipped her ever so gently, and her back arched off the bed, pushing herself closer to him. She'd never felt anything like what Rhett was making her feel.

Treasured. Desired. Loved.

His hand followed the trail of his lips and cupped her breast, bringing it to his mouth again before paying attention to its twin. She was lost in an ocean of pleasure as he continued his kisses down her body, dipping briefly into her navel and then over the softness of her belly.

"I love your belly," he said, kissing her there. He ran his hand over the dip at her waist and then the outward swell of her hip and down her thigh. "I love your hips. I love your thighs."

She moaned and closed her eyes at his words, tilting her head back on the pillow.

His hand danced over the flesh of her thigh before sliding between her legs. He groaned. "I love your beautiful pussy."

She flushed and writhed on the bed, his words turning her on more than she thought possible.

"You are so damned beautiful. I wish you could see yourself. All glowing and sexy."

He dropped his head between her thighs and the world outside this room—outside the two of them—ceased to exist. She was a mess of sighs and moans.

And the whole time he was licking and teasing her with his tongue and lips like he'd been lost in the desert for days and she was the first drop of rain.

# Chapter Sixteen

**Rhett**

He loved how Charlotte tasted. He couldn't get enough of her. When she came, she was completely unselfconscious, hands gripping the sheets and twisting, her head thrown back, her back arched. She did this little gasp and moan that was adorable, and he just wanted to see her come again and again.

He dropped a kiss to her stomach before pulling open the bedside drawer and fishing around for the box of condoms he knew he'd stashed in there.

"Do you want to keep going?" he asked her, and she nodded. He lifted a brow, and she caught herself.

"Yes, Rhett. I want you to fuck me," she said with a wicked twist to her lips.

He groaned, grabbing his dick and squeezing in an effort to hold back. "Shit."

She giggled as he attempted to maintain control, and he groaned again. She was a tease, and he loved it. He sat up and ripped open the brand new box and fished out a silver foil packet.

Charlotte was silent as she watched him, one arm thrown up over her head, her hair mussed from where she'd been twisting on the pillow. Her lips were puffy from his kisses, and there was that pink in her cheeks that he loved so much.

"You have no idea just how beautiful you are." He surged forward to claim her lips with his. This woman could destroy him. He was going to do everything in his power to make sure she never felt she had to.

Kissing her would never get old, he decided.

He'd be ninety and still want to kiss her.

He pulled back and ripped the foil packet open, then carefully rolled it down his length.

"Any final words?" he joked, and she laughed. The sound went straight to his heart.

"I was wondering when I was going to have my insides rearranged by that." She pointed to his groin.

"We don't have to—"

"Don't you dare! You don't wave a giant dick like that around in front of me and not let me ride it."

He barked out a laugh. Sure, his dick was a little longer than most—and a little thicker—but he'd make sure she felt good. He settled himself between her thighs, and met her eyes. "Yes?"

"One thousand times yes, Rhett. Please!" Her eyes were heated, and it wasn't his face she was looking at, but where their bodies would join.

He slid into her with a gentle push, being careful to not cause her any discomfort. She gasped, and he paused, halfway buried inside her gloriously tight wet heat and, breath catching in his throat, watched her face. He held still, fighting against the need to move, until she nodded. Then he slowly shifted his hips.

With each small thrust, she clung harder to him until her nails were digging into his back, but he didn't care. She was everything he ever wanted.

She was his life.

"You're so beautiful, Charlie," he told her as he worshipped her body with his own.

He took his time, pausing to kiss and tease her nipples, kissing her neck, touching her everywhere he could reach until she was a writhing mess beneath him.

As they moved closer and closer to joint oblivion, his heart finally felt whole.

He'd found the one person who completed him.

He was never letting her go.

"Oh god, Rhett!" she cried out as she shattered, arching her back. Her skin was flushed, her hair spread across the pillows. A goddess wouldn't have been as captivating as her in that moment.

He paused inside her, desperately trying to not topple over after her, but it was too late. With a growl, he slid a hand under her backside and chased his own release, finding it quickly after her with short, fast thrusts.

They were both breathing hard, sweat across their brows as he slowly pulled from her body and moved to the bathroom. He took care of the condom and grabbed a pair of wash cloths, warming them before heading back to the bedroom.

It was his pleasure to take care of her, and he said as much as he cleaned between her legs and then took care of himself.

She was drowsy and sated as he settled back into bed next to her, pulling the covers back up.

"Rhett?" she asked sleepily, curled on her side with her hand resting on his chest. He stroked her hair with one hand, the other stretching over the top of her.

"Hmm?"

She opened sleepy blue eyes and met his. "Thank you."

He smiled. "For what?"

She snuggled back into his chest, and he barely

heard her words as she drifted to sleep. "For showing me I belong in Cape Wilde. For loving me like I love you. For just being you."

He smiled and held her close, vowing to never let a day pass without telling her he loved her.

# Epilogue

## Charlie

Another summer was over. Rhett and Charlie had been working almost non-stop for the past few months, sorting out the finishing touches on the last cabins to be renovated. The eco-lodge had just been approved for development and Charlie's trust fund had come in handy to make some improvements to the business. Their original idea had expanded to include an education center, and Rhett's cousin, Mason, had shown an interest in getting involved.

Rhett had gone into equal partnership with Charlie in Wilde Outdoor Adventures, who in turn was incredibly busy with the office-based tasks and the eco-lodge project. Meanwhile, Rhett had taken on a local high-school student to help him with the rental gear and answering the influx of inquiries they'd gotten since a TikTok of Rhett chopping wood had gone viral.

Much to his horror, and Charlie's amusement, Cassie had bought a life-sized cutout of Rhett holding an axe and put it in the front office of Wilde Outdoor Adventures. Cassie and Charlie had even jokingly made shirts that had 'Ask Me How To Get Wilde Outdoors' printed on them, and Charlie had put them up for sale on their new website.

They sold out within 24 hours.

Charlie couldn't remember laughing so much as when she'd had to explain to Rhett that he was considered a thirst trap. He'd gone bright red and refused to answer the phone for a week. But the tee shirts continued to sell out every time they were re-stocked, along with postcards of the West men hiking in some of the more picturesque locations with captions like 'Putting the wild in Cape Wilde'. That one was on a particularly arty shot of Logan emerging from a lake without a shirt on.

But now they could finally take a day off together and headed to Cassie's house for dinner.

"Did you get back to your dad?" Rhett pulled up outside Cassie's house.

"Not yet," Charlie replied as Rhett tuned the truck's engine off. "I'm not sure what to say."

"He apologized."

Charlie snorted. "Yeah, after almost a year of trying to guilt me into going back to New York. I'm not sure I can forgive him." She'd told Rhett what she'd overheard that day when she'd listened at her father's office door. Rhett had understood why she didn't want to see her father, let alone spend Christmas with him like he'd asked.

Rhett nodded. "I'll support whatever decision you make."

"I know." She smiled and leaned over to kiss him, balancing the salad bowl she was holding on her lap.

Cassie's house was a cute, white-painted cottage that sat overlooking the ocean at the same end of town where Rhett and Charlie lived. Rhett climbed the stairs to the front porch carrying a cooler, Charlie following.

"Cassie?" He called out as he opened the unlocked front door.

"Out the back!"

They made their way through the house and out onto the deck. Charlie smiled at the scene that was so different from her family.

Mason had commandeered the BBQ, turning steaks with one hand while holding a beer in the other. He'd forgone his prosthetic leg for the evening and was leaning against the railing on the deck while he worked, crutches propped up within easy reach.

Logan and Rowan were looking at the steps leading down to the garden, arguing over some maintenance work Logan thought was necessary before winter, and Rowan was trying to convince him it wasn't.

Amy, the family matriarch, was trying to help, but Cassie kept gesturing for her mother to sit down and relax.

Rhett put down the cooler. "Hey everyone."

Mason lifted a hand, the brief tilt to his lips the closest thing to a smile Charlie had ever seen on his face. Logan nodded and turned to Rowan, who dashed up the stairs to throw his arms around Charlie and Rhett both.

"Cousins!" Rowan cried with his usual bouncy enthusiasm before squeezing them hard enough that Rhett groaned. Laughing, Rowan bounded away to grab a beer.

Charlie coughed. "We're not cousins."

"Close enough," Rowan said, shaking Rhett's hand and patting him on the back before turning to kiss Charlie on the cheek.

Cassie brought Charlie a glass of white wine that she swapped for the salad bowl before claiming a seat at the table.

A gentle breeze blew, the last of the summer warmth dropping with the sun. The long, gauzy curtains that flank the French doors stirred gently.

"It feels like years since I just sat and relaxed," Rhett groaned as he sat next to Charlie and draped an arm over the back of the seat behind her.

"I know, right?" she laughed.

The sound of the water lapping against the rocks and the surrounding conversation soothed. She took a deep breath of the sea air and smiled, closing her eyes as she exhaled. She didn't miss New York one bit.

"That good, huh?" Rhett's deep rumble made her smile even wider.

"Yeah," she said simply.

"Love you, beautiful," he said, dropping a kiss to her temple.

"Love you too, big guy."

Thank you for reading Wilde Sanctuary by Melanie Hepburn!

If you enjoyed this book (and I really hope you did) please consider leaving a rating or a review on your preferred retail site.

As an independently published author every review and rating is very much appreciated.

If you'd like to keep in touch, join Melanie's newsletter at
melaniehepburn.com/list

The Cape Wilde Series continues with Logan West in Wilde Secrets. Read on for more...

# Wilde Secrets

By Melanie Hepburn

A big mistake that will cost a talented songwriter more than just her career. The broken-hearted, small town loner who rescues her from a storm. An attraction they both struggle to deny.

When Harper Holden accidentally destroys her entire life in one night, she does the only thing she can. She runs.

Straight into the muscular arms of flannel-clad carpenter Logan West.

The Cape Wilde loner does not want to play babysitter to a curvy runaway he rescues from a storm. But there's something about Harper that resurrects Logan's long-dormant protective instincts.

For Harper to get her life back, she must write the

best album of her life... in just three weeks. Or it won't just be her own career that is ruined. Logan decides to help, rallying the townspeople of Cape Wilde to support Harper in her hour of need.

But as the deadline looms, Harper realizes she has to make the biggest decision of her life. If she leaves Cape Wilde she'll get her career—and her life—back... but she'll lose her chance at a love of a lifetime.

Get Wilde Secrets now!
https://geni.us/wilde1

# About the Author

Melanie Hepburn is an Australian author of small town romances with strong, often curvy, women and the rugged outdoorsy men who can't get enough of them. She loves nothing more than sharing stories that'll make you laugh, swoon, and maybe blush just a little. Or maybe a lot. She make no promises.

When she's not writing she's reading or knitting (often at the same time) and avoiding housework. Melanie lives in Western Australia with her husband, their rescued greyhound and a cockatiel with more personality than he has any right to.

To keep in touch sign up for Melanie's newsletter on her website:

melaniehepburn.com/list

goodreads.com/melaniehepburn

bookbub.com/authors/melanie-hepburn

amazon.com/stores/author/B0DRZQ8CS1

# Thank you

I started writing this story in mid-2024 when I returned to indie publishing after 18 months of burnout. I have six other titles in another romance sub-genre, but wanted to try something new.

So here I am, writing small town coastal romances with rugged men who adore their strong women.

Thanks are due to the entire discord crew (you know who you are) for being an amazing support, for joining me in sprints, and not holding back in critiques.

The wonderful Courtney Fanning, challenged me to figure out what I really wanted to write.

My editor, Shana, whose considered advice is always spot on. Thanks for making me sound more American!

And last, but not least, my husband of ten years who will simply be known as Mr Hepburn. Thank you for insisting on proofing my books—even the spicy bits—and always being so proud of me. I love you more than chocolate.

Melanie xx

*February 2025*

# By Melanie Hepburn